LONG SHOT

BY

MARIE FOWLER

www.scobre.com

Scobre Press Corporation
2255 Calle Clara
La Jolla, CA 92307

Scobre Press books may be purchased for educa-
tional, business or sales promotional use.

First Scobre edition published 2003.

Edited by Ramey Temple & Michael Fisher
Illustrated by Larry Salk
Cover Design by Michael Lynch

ISBN 0-9741997-0-2

HOME RUN EDITION

www.scobre.com

CHAPTER ONE

THE LIST

"Put it up!" I screamed, as Clarissa drove past two defenders. She released a hook shot over the top of Tree Hastings. Tree was our close friend and the biggest guy on campus. Her rainbow arched high above his outstretched arms and passed through the orange rim. Swish! The sweet sound of nothing but net.

Pick-up games——that's all that remained of my final college season. Of course, these weren't just ordinary pick-up games. We played two-on two against some guys we were friends with. They weren't great, but they made up for a lack of talent with size.

"Shoot!" Clarissa and I yelled, trying to rattle Rob Coker. He always dribbled between his legs for no reason and smiled at us. I slapped the ball away

1

from him. "Get real, Rob." He thought he could beat us. Plus, he'd ask me out after almost every game. It was really annoying.

My jumper kissed off the glass and dropped through the hoop. "Twenty-six, all!" I called out.

Rob was still talking trash. "Is that all you've got, Brit?" He shifted left at the last minute, expecting to leave me flatfooted. But I anticipated him and snatched the ball.

When I got to the three-point line, Rob jumped past me. This left me with a wide open look at the basket. I calmly flipped the ball toward the hoop; nothing but net. "That's three, Robbie."

"That's luck, Brit."

"That's game, guys," Clarissa laughed. "Good thing too, 'cause I'm getting pretty hungry."

When we played against the guys, the prize was always dinner. "I think I feel like burgers tonight," I said from the three-point line. I shot one more swish and looked over at Rob. "I guess that was luck, too." I knew how to handle these guys. I had an older brother and played plenty of basketball against the boys.

It was early April. March Madness was long forgotten. The World University Games in Mexico City were just a pleasant memory. Today was a big day for my basketball career. I was about to find out about the Olympic team, and whether or not I'd been invited to try out. I'd been nervous all day. All I wanted *was a chance.*

After four years, I was about to leave the University of Northern Virginia. What was next—I had no idea. My teammates all had their engines revving for the future. I was stuck in neutral. Ming was going to start graduate school at Long Island State. Andrea was getting married. Clarissa was headed to the WNBA. My other teammates had a year or so left before they graduated.

I was a twenty-two-year-old, five-foot-three-inch point guard. My jumper was great, but it wasn't enough to impress pro scouts. I hadn't been drafted, but I had hope. I would try out for a WNBA team even though no team had chosen me. I packed my stuff and left to pick up my camera for photography class. Clarissa stuck around to find out who'd been invited to Olympic tryouts.

I bounced a ball everywhere I went on campus. The more I dribbled, the better my handle was. As a point guard, your ability to dribble the ball is everything. You have to be in total control or your entire team will crumble. You're the leader on the floor, the eyes, ears, and heart of your team. I loved playing point guard. The choices I made on every play affected the game. If I wanted to run, we ran. If I slowed it down, we'd dig in our heels and bang inside. I was the captain, the lead singer, the quarterback, the pilot, the pitcher, the—

"Brittany, wait up!" A voice came from be-

hind me, breaking my thoughts.

I slowed my dribble. Clarissa was racing up the walk to catch me. She was out of breath. "I got the word on tryouts," she shouted with a new burst of energy. "Los Angeles! Middle of June!" A player had to be specifically asked to attend the Olympic trials. While I was sure Clarissa would be invited, I doubted that I would. "Come on," she said, tugging at my arm. "Coach has the list."

We raced back to the locker room and the invite list. Coach Hollins had tacked it onto the bulletin board. I was nervous as Clarissa quickly scanned it. She was always one to confront things head on. Me, I wanted it so badly that I was afraid to look.

"We're in." Clarissa shouted, giving me a hug.

"We?" I asked, looking at her like she was crazy.

"We're going to LA!" she yelled. The purple beads braided into her dark hair bounced around as she shook her head. Clarissa read, "Los Angeles, California, June 15, to try out for," she paused for effect. "The United States Olympic Basketball Team!" she screamed these words.

I couldn't believe my ears. I snatched the list away from her so I could see for myself. Sure enough, there I was—Brittany Bristol, Northern Virginia. How about that?

"Who else made it?" Clarissa asked, looking over my shoulder. "Starling!" she gasped. I nodded.

4

Sherry Sterling, my biggest rival since high school, would be trying out too. Clarissa was my closest friend, but even she couldn't resist being amused. "Better watch the room assignments, Brit. Starling'll be after you."

We called her "Starling" after a flock of pitch-black birds that had plagued our campus. We gave her this nickname during the fall of my junior year. Everything the groundskeepers did to discourage the birds seemed to entice more of them to come. They were everywhere, and the starlings got blamed for everything bad that happened on campus.

So when we heard the name "Sherry Sterling," "Starling" was just a natural. It helped that she had long, dark hair, too. On the court, Sherry would stoop to any dirty trick in the book. There was no reason for it either because she was a really good player. Still, Sherry would fake an injury the minute the momentum swung against her team. Or she would trip a player as she drove toward the basket. That kind of thing got to all of us, but most of all to me. It was probably because I'd known her the longest. I had to deal with Sherry when she played for our high school rival, Shenandoah.

And then there was the matter of Brian, my brother Eric's best friend. I adored Brian from the time I could do nothing but tag along after him. By junior year, he was the great love of my life. He didn't know this, of course. I was nothing more than Eric's kid sister to him. Anyway, Sherry and Brian, well —

I was brought back from my daydreaming again by Clarissa, "Time to celebrate, Brit."

I left Starling and Brian in the back of my head. We sat down in Everett Hall, the cafeteria I'd been eating in for the past four years. Clarissa and I were going to be trying out for the Olympic team! At least fifteen others joined us in our celebration.

The University of Northern Virginia is a small school outside of Washington, D.C. It wasn't too far from Oak Grove, Virginia, where I grew up. I've had a lot of great times here. I've had some tough times too and I've grown up a lot. That happens no matter what, I suppose, but UNV was the place it happened to me.

We ordered the Special, a campus favorite. It was twelve scoops of different kinds of ice cream smothered in hot fudge. This would be our last splurge before getting into our training for tryouts. Everyone hovered around to get a bite. Jen and Andrea leaned in from one side, while Tree and Rob reached in from the other. Rob nudged in so close he nearly knocked me off my stool.

I spaced out, daydreaming again, while everyone around me talked and ate. I fantasized about competing in the Olympics. I even imagined winning a gold medal for my country. "Wake up, Brit!" Clarissa hit me on the wrist with her spoon. "Strawberry's about gone."

I dug back into the ice cream quickly. Strawberry ice cream was my favorite, while Clarissa's favorite was vanilla. Like good buddies, we looked out for one another. Looking back, it's pretty amazing that we ended up best friends. We certainly didn't start out very friendly when we came to UNV. I came in just hoping to be on the team. Clarissa came in expecting to be the star. Or at least that's what we all thought. It took her a long time to warm up to people when she first arrived.

We've always been very different, especially on the basketball court. Clarissa is tall. She plays center and has an incredible hook shot. Coach says her hook is as good as anyone's, college or pro, male or female. I'm a little point guard, a playmaker, more than a pure shooter. I'm not big, and I don't have much speed or a wide variety of shots. In fact, people are always amazed when they discover that I'm a basketball player.

My one great beauty is my long reddish-blonde hair. It took me a while to grow it out just perfectly. I finally got it right during my junior year. Not that I'm a cover girl, but guys are surprised to learn that I'm an athlete. (Why do they always think cute girls can't play sports?)

What I have going for me is that I "keep my head in the game." And hey, I'm a good foul shooter, an underappreciated skill. During my last season I hit one hundred and three free throws in a row. That set a new school record, a new conference record, and even an NCAA record.

Of course, my brother Eric claims he and Brian should get credit for my skills. They let me practice with them when I was younger. If I missed a foul shot, I couldn't touch the ball for the next five minutes. They took turns driving at the basket, making me work to stop them. In the beginning, I think it was their way of trying to get rid of me. But I was too stubborn for that. So I became an excellent free-throw shooter, and got pretty good at defending.

I glanced at my watch. "I've got to run. Photography class." I stood and Leesha thrust a basketball at me. "Don't waste time, Brit, dribble everywhere."

I hesitated, but Clarissa made a comment that changed my mind. "You know Starling's dribbling somewhere right now." She probably was.

I took the ball and bounced my way toward Patriot Hall, the fine arts building. I probably spent as much time there as I did in Hamilton Gym. I came to college wanting to be a great painter like Georgia O'Keeffe. I was fascinated by those big, beautiful flowers that filled her canvases. I spent hours copying her works and drew hundreds of flowers myself.

Unfortunately, I wasn't very good at drawing. My teacher suggested I try photography. Since I still loved flowers, I photographed hundreds of them in gardens. In the end, I discovered that I loved photography, and not painting. It's funny how life happens that way sometimes. You think you know what you want; then you find out what you really want by accident.

I guess I became a basketball player in the same way. I spent so many hours playing basketball with Eric and Brian. But it wasn't because I loved the game, I just wanted to be included. I didn't care about basketball half as much as I cared about them noticing me. Who would have guessed it would end up being so important to me?

I passed by the fountain in the center of campus. Students would always toss in a coin and make a wish. I looked in my pockets. The only coin I had was my lucky Washington State quarter. There was no way I could throw that one away. It had been bringing me good luck since high school. I walked past the fountain without dropping any money in. Oh well, I was going to Los Angeles to try out for the Olympics! What more could I wish for anyway?

Looking back on my life from where I am now is really strange. Sometimes, I think about how I got here. This whole thing started back in high school, out in front of Brian's house.

CHAPTER TWO

A NATURAL

I had to walk home from high school every day during my freshman year. I had to wait another year before getting my driver's license. But I grew to love my walks, especially in the fall, when the October sky was bright blue and crystal clear. On these days, I wouldn't take the quickest route home. On my "short-cut," I would eventually hear the bouncing of a basketball. My brother Eric and his best friend Brian would be playing one-on-one. Secretly, their game was the reason I went this way to begin with. I knew they'd be outside shooting hoops. They always were.

Brian had a dog, a brown and white terrier named Max. He would always be the first to greet me when I stopped by the driveway. Naturally, the boys usually pretended they didn't see me. Every chance I got, I would try to play in their games. One day, after a few minutes of petting Max, I decided I wanted to play with the boys. So I turned my attention toward the game. It didn't take long before an errant pass came my way. I snagged it and dribbled a few times.

"Come on, Brit, give it back," Eric shouted.

I ignored my brother, grinning at him while I dribbled. "Can I play?" I asked.

"Get lost," Eric ordered, refusing to glance in my direction.

I dribbled the ball again, but Brian ran toward me and stole it. His eyes met mine. I looked away. Brian dribbled the ball to the end of the driveway and looked at Eric. "Make it from here or your sister plays," he shouted.

I smiled at Brian.

Eric made an annoyed face. He knew it was nearly impossible to make a shot from way back there. He let it fly anyway. The ball bounced off the top of the backboard and I raced forward to catch it.

"Fine, two-on-one," Eric shouted. My heart sunk for a moment. It didn't take a genius to figure out who the "one" would be. I didn't care though, I was playing. That's all I wanted anyway.

I knew that stealing the ball would be my best chance at a shot. So I kept my hands loose and ready. After only a couple of possessions, I slapped the ball away from Eric. "You're not bad, Brit," Brian said. "You should try out for the girls' team."

I was surprised by this comment. But since it came from Brian, I didn't shrug it off. The girls' team? I'd never really given that any thought. I gazed at Brian. Just looking at his blue eyes made my heart skip a beat. Eric was there quickly to ruin my moment. "Yeah, like she has a chance," he said, trying to steal the ball.

I stepped away from them and took a poorly aimed shot. It bounced past the garage and into a rose bush. Max chased it down, barking all the way.

Brian finally retrieved the ball. "You've got to work on that shot, though," he said softly. Then he shouted, "Let's play horse, Eric."

"Not again," Eric groaned.

Brian insisted. "We have to help your sister out. She needs a lot of work if she expects to make the team." Brian was trying to include me and I had no idea why. I stared at him and our eyes met a second time.

Eric shouted, "Well, stop staring at each other and lets play."

Brian blushed, embarrassed, "I wasn't staring at her." He threw up a shot.

I tried to smile over at Brian. Unfortunately, he didn't really look at me the rest of the game. Still, I felt excited about trying out for the girls' team. I was especially excited that Brian was helping me.

We played until Brian's mom called him in for supper. Then Eric and I walked home, taking turns dribbling. He always treated me better when I was the only one around. "So how's freshman year going?" he asked. He bounced the ball off of a fence near Smith Clove Park.

"So far, so good," I answered. "Math's OK, English, too. But I really like physics."

Eric made a face. "That's only because you're good at drawing stuff. I couldn't wait to get out of there."

A car passed and the horn honked. Eric waved.

"Who's that?" I asked. I knew he'd never volunteer the information.

"Susan Ambler," he mumbled.

"The cheerleader?"

"Yeah."

I rolled my eyes. "Don't tell me you're interested in her? She's got to be the most stuck-up person in the whole school." None of the girls at Jefferson High could bear Susan Ambler. She probably didn't have a single girlfriend. Then again, she didn't need us. It was sickening how the boys tripped over each other for her. And now my brother was falling for her! This was just too much.

"Hey," Eric scolded, "she's cool. Besides, it's Brian she likes."

"Don't tell me that Brian—" I stopped myself. I was more annoyed now, than I was when I thought she liked Eric. I couldn't bear the thought of her and Brian together.

He nodded. "He talks to her all the time."

I kicked at a rock in frustration. Eric broke the silence. "Why do you care?"

"I don't. I was just——"

Eric cut me off, "I'll race you home." He took off, knowing he'd caught me off guard. I gave chase, but he still beat me out by a hair.

Tryouts for the junior varsity girls' team took place in October. Junior varsity, or JV, was a high school team comprised of freshman and sophomores. I was extra nervous because I hadn't played any school sports before. I didn't know what to expect. Eric and Brian had driven me crazy working on free throws since I was twelve. So I hoped that part of tryouts would go well. Still, I was sure I couldn't possibly make the team. There were about forty girls trying out for just fifteen spots.

I wore my lucky tee shirt from Virginia Beach and laced up my high tops. The guy in charge of the JV team was Coach Buzz Holt. He was a Jefferson graduate who went on to play at Duane University. When he arrived, Coach threw a bunch of basketballs onto the court. His deep voice commanded us to warm up. Coach then divided us into squads to run drills. We spent an hour dribbling and passing up and down the court, back and forth. Then we formed lines for lay up drills, right handed and left. Coach took a bunch of black electrical tape and made marks all over the court. We were supposed to dribble to each mark and fire a shot without hesitation. This was something I'd never practiced. I soon learned that shooting off the dribble was more difficult than a set jumper.

Coach watched this drill carefully. I dribbled the ball off of my toe on the first shot. But after that, I made about half my shots. This put me in the middle of pack. Our last drill was shooting free throws, where I always looked good. I made 7 of the 10 shots I took. I was glad this was the last thing Coach saw me do before sitting us down in the bleachers.

"Y'all are real good, so give yourselves a round of applause." He began his speech with a broad smile and a thick southern accent. Everyone applauded, but the tension in the air remained thick. I sat in the top row, fidgeting uncontrollably. "Anyway, I'd like to take another look at some of you before I pick. If I call your name, come back tomorrow and we'll go through the drills again." He paused a moment. "If I don't call your name, thank you for coming out. Keep practicing and try again next year."

Suddenly I wished I hadn't worn a bright orange tee shirt. I wanted to be invisible. I thought Coach would post his choices on the bulletin board or something. I didn't want to find out in front of everybody! I could feel my face getting redder and redder. My head must have looked like a giant cherry tomato. Coach's lips kept moving but I couldn't hear a word he said. Suddenly, Jessica Bergman, the girl sitting beside me, slapped my knee. "Way to go, Brit," she whispered.

I swallowed. Had he really called my name? Relief began to wash over me. My ears opened up and I could hear again. "Tyson, Walker, and Wells. That's it. Thanks for your time, girls."

I couldn't believe I'd made the first cut. Maybe I wasn't that bad after all. While changing in the locker room, the sophomores treated me with a new respect. I couldn't wait to tell Eric and Brian. I left the locker room and headed straight for Brian's house.

The boys were more surprised than I was that I got asked back. I guess that says a lot about what they really thought of my ability. The three of us worked on my jump shot and other drills from tryouts. Finally, we sat down, exhausted. "If you make the team, Brit, you really owe us," Eric said.

"You got it." I was so tired I could hardly keep my eyes from closing.

The night ended when Brian's mother told him he had a telephone call. With that, he stood up and said goodnight. Just before he left, I caught him wink over at Eric. I knew what that meant—Susan Ambler was on the phone.

Mom washed my lucky Virginia Beach shirt so I could wear it the next day for tryouts. By the time I got out of ninth period, most of the girls were already shooting. A crowd of older students hung around the gym, looking in on the tryout. Eric was there, too. He was waving at me encouragingly. Wow, he actually acknowledged me in front of his friends.

Coach Holt put us through the same drills as the day before. We had to run around the court until I was sure I would pass out. Worse, I saw Brian and Susan Ambler walk over to Eric. I stumbled, but caught myself and kept running. Susan always made me feel clumsy.

Free throws were next. I redid the orange scrunchee holding back my hair. I was letting it grow and it wouldn't stay back by itself. Mostly, it hung down in stringy wet strands. I didn't mind that too much. We weren't supposed to be models, we were playing basketball. Still, when I saw Susan with her perfect blonde hair, I felt like a klutz. I was sweating. She was cool and neat and beautiful. I tried to focus on the free throws. Calm down, Brit, I told myself.

I shot five free throws and wasn't close on any of them. Something was wrong. I always made my free throws. Susan had rattled me. I hoped Coach Holt hadn't seen me throw those clunkers.

A few minutes later, Coach blew the whistle and we gathered in the bleachers. Up until my free throws, I had felt fairly confident. I even thought I'd played better than yesterday. Coach began with the same message as the day before: "At your age a lot can change in a year. So don't be too discouraged if you don't make the team." Yeah right, I thought to myself. "I have to admit," Coach continued, "it was really hard deciding. I did the best I could." He glanced down at the clipboard in his hand. "Every one of you is a winner just for trying."

Coach began by calling out the sophomores. No surprises there. They had all played on the team last year. He started in on the freshman and I had a funny feeling in my stomach. I listened impatiently, waiting to hear my name. When he finished speaking, I was motionless. My name hadn't been called. I didn't make the team. My stomach was now feeling really sick and my face felt hot. Everybody in the gym seemed to be staring at me. I suddenly wished Eric and Brian hadn't come, and especially Susan Ambler.

All around me, girls were giving each other high fives, shrieking and hugging. I stumbled down from my seat, still in shock. I couldn't face the happy locker room. So I raced out through a side exit and shot down the sidewalk toward home. At first, I hadn't really expected to make the team. But after yesterday, I let myself think that maybe I had a chance. Hot tears stung my eyes, but I refused to cry. Somebody might see me and discover how much I actually cared.

It took a while to get over my disappointment. At first, I blamed it all on Susan Ambler. She broke my concentration. If she hadn't showed up, I'd have made those foul shots and made the team. Then I blamed Coach Holt. He should have seen what a good player I was. None of these theories made me feel any better about not making the team. In the end, I resigned myself to trying again next season.

Naturally, I didn't want anything to do with the

girls who made the team. OK, I admit it, I was bitter. Then a couple of them ended up being in my math class. We got to know each other and I started going to some of their games. Eric and Brian were both on the boy's team and had little time for me. So I got in the habit of cheering for the girls' JV.

And when the team's scorekeeper got sick, I filled in for her. I got to know the players better and learned a lot about basketball, too. After a few games, I started seeing basketball in a different way. I was noticing passing lanes and could read what other defenses were doing. I even knew where the ball should be, and who should get it. Most of the girls never thought about basketball this way. At halftime I would always tell Coach Holt all the things I'd noticed. He loved hearing my advice and often used it to help us win. Coach Holt called me a natural. He said that some day I would make a great coach.

But I didn't want to be a natural or a coach— I wanted to play.

CHAPTER THREE

LAYOVER

"Flight attendants, please prepare for arrival."

I leaned against the window of the plane, gazing at the golden California mountains. San Francisco and a long layover—I would have to kill four hours before my connecting flight. Then, it was off to Los Angeles and Olympic trials.

Once Clarissa and I got the word on the tryouts, everything went fast. The season ended, I took my finals and graduated. It's funny how time whizzes by when things are going well. Before I knew it, I was packing my bags for Los Angeles.

"The temperature here in San Francisco is sixty eight degrees with sunny skies. We thank you for flying with us and hope to see you again soon." *The pilot's voice brought me back to reality.*

Once again, I felt guilty that Clarissa wasn't here with me. Her Achilles tendon was injured and the doctors insisted she skip the trials. I was living out our dream without her. She desperately wanted to play in the Olympics, but the danger of a career threatening injury was just too great.

I'd never been to San Francisco and had planned to do some sightseeing. Impatient to start, I fiddled with my seat belt. The plane was rolling slowly toward the terminal. I had my carry-on bag in hand. It was carefully turned so people could see the words "US Olympic Trials." I was proud of the red white and blue letters printed on my bag.

A few minutes later, I entered the terminal. I folded up my city map and placed it in my pocket. Then I headed straight for the baggage lockers. Ok, put a couple of quarters in the slot. Careful, Brit, not your lucky Washington one. Turn the key and here we go. Whenever I talked to myself, I knew I was nervous.

I glanced down at my wrist, changing my watch to Pacific time. The tiny little knob was impossible to turn. I wasn't looking where I was going while I fiddled with my watch. Of course, I stumbled into someone by accident. Flustered, I began to apologize. "I'm sorry I——" Then my heart stopped.

The young naval officer spoke in a deep voice. "Are you OK?" he asked.

I was speechless. He was more handsome than

I remembered. "Brian," I finally managed to say.

His light blue eyes crinkled and a smile came to his face. "Brittany?" he asked, shaking his head. He laughed in disbelief, looking me up and down. "Is that really you? I haven't seen you in like five years."

I nodded, trying to look older and more composed.

He gave me a quick hug. "Wow! You look great."

I was definitely blushing. "You too." I paused, in shock. " So what are you doing here, Brian?" I blurted out nervously.

"Well, flying, obviously." He laughed in the same slightly sarcastic teasing way that I remembered. "I'm headed up to Bremerton, Washington. You?"

"I'm, uh, headed to Los Angeles," I stammered.

"Oh that's too bad," he said. I heard regret in his voice. "I'm passing through and I've got a long layover." Great place to be held up, though. San Francisco's just about my favorite city in the world." His blue eyes found me again.

I hesitated before speaking. I was sure Brian had a girlfriend and I didn't want to seem pushy. Oh, what the heck, I thought. "I actually have a few hours too." I smiled.

His voice brightened. "Well, how about I show

you around? You always needed a little instruction, anyway." He was awkward when he said, "If you're up for it, I mean."

Was I up for it? Was I ever! I tried to be nonchalant. "I guess. I mean, if you have the time," I shrugged casually.

He snatched up his brown duffel bag and we walked out under a clear blue sky. "Let's see if the rental company will give a navy guy a convertible."

Brian was as good as his word. In no time, we were in the front seat of a red Mustang. "This is a bit different than my jet," he said with a sly grin. "I'll try to keep it under control." He turned the key and revved the engine.

"You always wanted to fly, Brian." I remembered back to when we were kids. How I'd steal the ball from him every time a jet flew overhead. I got to be good at picking up the sound of a jet engine. Any time one flew overhead, Brian couldn't keep his head from straying to the sky.

The summer after freshman year, I played basketball every day. Dad put a hoop up over our garage door so I could practice at home. Before I knew it, school started up again. Eric and Brian were juniors, so they were pretty busy with upperclassmen stuff. But we still played basketball every afternoon. I could tell I was getting better too. I liked spotting up from the top of the key. I decided that this was my spot. When left opened from there, I rarely missed. I practiced this shot all the time until it was nearly unstoppable. My training also included push-ups and sit-ups. Occasionally, I'd even lift some of Eric's weights. I was much faster and stronger than a year earlier.

I entered the JV tryouts with a newfound confidence. I walked into the gym with my chin up. I passed with great velocity. I shot without hesitating. And I ran Coach Holts drills as if I'd been practicing them all summer. The truth was—I had been.

After the standard drills, Coach threw us a curve. He divided us up into four teams to play shortened games. This was totally unexpected. He then introduced four guys from the boys' varsity team. They would be our squad coaches for the day. I lucked out because Brian volunteered to coach my team. He told me I'd be playing point guard, the position I wanted to play. Even Coach Holt had told me I had "the right brain" for a point guard.

When Coach blew his whistle to start play, I was really nervous. My palms were sweating and my heart was racing. Luckily, one of the girls on my squad was Kendra Grant. She had been the team's leading scorer the year before. My strategy was to toss her the ball as often as possible. A good point guard gets the ball to her best scorers when they have opportunities to score. This was the simple philosophy I kept in mind.

It took a few runs up and down the court before anyone made a shot. In the first game, I thought I did OK. I found open players and made sharp passes. But the games were so short. It was hard to tell what Coach noticed and what he missed.

I paid close attention to the games when I was on the bench. Other girls sat around and talked, but I really focused. This was my chance to see things that could give me a leg up when it was my turn to play again. I noticed that some players were real ball hogs. Others were afraid of the ball altogether. They were probably scared of making a mistake. I could tell that a few were even concerned about not breaking a fingernail! I had my whole life to grow pretty fingernails. Right now, the game was all that mattered.

Coach blew his whistle again, and Brian sent me back in to play. I was the point guard once again, controlling the ball. I dribbled confidently, head up, eyes scanning the court. This was my natural position and I could just feel it. From that day forward, if I was playing basketball, I was playing point guard.

Kendra was ready, and I quickly fired a pass into her hands. She grabbed it and put it in the basket all in one motion. One play, one pass, one assist.

Now on defense, I put pressure on the guard bringing the ball up. I may be small, but I'm smart and scrappy. I'd seen how tight defense made her uneasy in the last game. I gave her little breathing space. She was out of control and forced a bad pass down low. My teammate intercepted it easily. There was no way she was getting that one in there.

The ball came my way and I faked a shot from the three-point arc. Sharon Nichols fell for it, leaving her feet and leaping into the air. Without her in my way, I tossed a bounce pass to Kendra again. She put it up off the window and was fouled in the process. She missed her free throw and Jan Wilson grabbed the rebound. Right away, Jan tried to make a long pass to a teammate.

I read her eyes and reached high into the air. The ball skipped off my fingertips and right back into Kendra's hands. She nailed another ten-footer off the backboard. Her basket capped off my best five minutes of the tryouts, especially defensively.

When the whistle blew, we sat down and grabbed some water. By the time I finished my cup, the tryout was over. Coach Holt called us together for the first cut.

I was pretty sure I'd made it, and I was right. I was now one step closer to making the team.

I raced over to Brian's house after school. "You looked pretty good out there, Brit," Brian smiled. He slapped Eric on the back. "You'd have been impressed, man." Eric just rolled his eyes.

I had a free period before tryouts the next day, so I lounged around the gym, taking an occasional warm-up shot. My hair had gotten longer and Kendra braided it for me. "We've been talking about the whole team braiding our hair for the season." Kendra confided this to me as she neatly tied the end of a braid. I sighed, not sure what to say. I didn't want to jinx myself. Kendra knew what I was thinking and grinned. "Come on, Brittany, you're going to make it."

Before I could respond, Brian walked up, "I found this on the sidewalk." He held out a quarter in the palm of his hand. "It just came out, it's the Washington one." He flipped it to me. "Maybe it'll bring you luck."

I slipped the quarter in my pocket and went out onto the court. Coach Holt arrived, and put every girl through the skills drills again. I had another good day of tryouts, playing smart basketball.

When Coach announced his choices, I made sure not to get my hopes up. I took a seat way in the back. No one would see my quick exit if I got cut this time. Across the gym, Brian gave me a thumbs up. I rubbed the quarter in my pocket for good luck.

This time, after a year of waiting, Coach called out, "Brittany Bristol..." I shot out of my seat like a rocket. There was yelling and screaming and whoops of joy all around me. I was on the team.

Caught up in my good fortune, I could think of nothing else. I floated to the locker room and gathered up my things. When I headed out to the main hallway, I hoped to see Brian.

I saw him all right, standing in a corner locking lips with Susan Ambler. He didn't even look up, but I wasn't about to let that spoil my day.

CHAPTER FOUR

LOSING IT

I sat comfortably in the front seat, positioning myself to face Brian. This was my first time in a convertible. Besides the tricks it played with my hair, I liked it.

"How's Eric?" Brian asked, as we pulled onto the freeway.

"He's good," I said. "Just got accepted to vet school at Ohio College. Must be Mad Max's influence," I laughed, remembering Brian's terrier.

He smiled at the thought of Max. Then he stared off for a second. "Is Eric still seeing——um, what was her name?" he prodded. "You know who I mean, the cheerleader with blonde hair."

"Susan Ambler." I was none too pleased to be reminded of her. "I'm surprised you could forget her,

Brian. The two of you were inseparable."

"Until she decided she liked your brother."
He laughed, unaffected. After all, from what I'd
heard, Brian replaced Susan with darling Starling.

"Fortunately for Eric, they're no longer a
couple." I hope my voice didn't sound too bitter. "He's
seeing a girl, but I don't think it's too serious." I was
dying to know about Brian's love life, but I tried to
seem casual. "And you? Are you still seeing Sherry
Sterling?" I had a hard time hiding my feelings for
Sherry.

Brian noticed how uncomfortable I'd just gotten. "You never liked Sherry much, did you?" he
asked.

I couldn't lie to him. "Well, not really."

"She's a great girl, Brit, just misunderstood.
Boy has she had it rough." Yeah right, I thought,
not knowing how to respond. Brian broke into my
thoughts, grinning. "To answer your question——I'm
single. Sailor's don't settle down that easily."

"So you're not dating Sherry?" I needed a
confirmation here.

"No," he said. I cracked a small smile, half
confused, half delighted. "Anyway, you haven't told
me why you're headed to LA."

I tried to keep the pride from my voice. "I'm
trying out for the Women's Olympic basketball team,"
I said.

"No kidding?" Brian looked shocked. "Wow!

Good for you, Brit!" He gave a low whistle. "I had no idea you were that good."

"I'm not really," I said modestly.

"And you're so little, too. You must have a heck of a jumper, huh?"

"It's OK," I confessed.

"Well, you must be pretty great to try out for the Olympics. That's something else, Brit." Brian was definitely impressed. He turned his attention back to the traffic as the city stood in front of us. I dug out my camera and snapped away while he looked for a parking space.

I couldn't deny the thrill of excitement as I looked at the red cable cars climbing up the steep hills. I guess it was the hills that jogged my memory and I started to laugh.

"What's so funny?" Brian looked mystified.

"Remember the time you had your Dad's car on Skyline Drive?" The image of Eric, myself, and a few other kids packed into a station wagon was clear. I started to laugh, remembering how it died and we had to push it the whole way home..

"Yeah, I got on the wrong road giving you a ride home. Then I ran out of gas. Nice memory, Brit." Brian groaned.

As a member of the JV team, I played hard. I gave everything I had every practice. But I wasn't good enough to be a starter. It hurt sitting on the bench. Worse, Christine Davis, the girl who started instead of me, played almost every minute.

Being on the sidelines made analyzing our games easier. My conclusion was that we were simply too selfish out there. The concept of "team" was constantly adjusted depending on who was on the floor. This was true off the court as well. The other starters tended to only hang out with each other. I tried not to care, but it was hard. All five of them were sophomores, my classmates. Still, they didn't include me because I was a bench player. It didn't matter to them that we were in the same grade. Being the only non-freshman who wasn't starting made me feel awkward.

One day, Christine didn't come to school until fourth period. Coach Holt had a rule: if you're not in school all day, you don't play. No exceptions. Coach told her right away that she couldn't dress for the game.

We were playing rival Shenandoah in a crucial contest. My chance had finally arrived. I was in the starting lineup. I tried to stay calm, telling myself that this was a game like any other. But that wasn't close to the truth. Today I would be on the hardwood floor instead of the bench.

By tip-off, I was a bag of nerves. I bobbled the first ball that was passed to me. It skittered off my foot and slammed against the bleachers. Out of bounds. Way to start the game off, Brit.

On defense, I got ready to guard their wiry and explosive guard, Sherry Sterling. I had never seen

Sherry before. This game marked the beginning of our rivalry. I reached out to disrupt her dribble, but no success. She flicked the ball behind her back and changed direction. I was off balance one minute and flat on my back the next. I had never defended such a skilled ball handler. She scored easily before I got to my feet again.

Audrey passed the ball to me and my heart was pounding. I was determined to do well, but I fired a pass too high to Kendra. The ball bounced off her hands, out of bounds.

Coach quickly called a time-out. "Settle down, Brit," he said in the huddle. "You've got way too much adrenaline."

Kendra and Audrey both glared at me. Christine, sitting on the bench, rolled her eyes and sighed. I drank some water and resolved to do better.

I wanted to keep it simple for the rest of the half. So I focused on getting the ball to Kendra and Audrey. My strategy worked and we managed to go to the locker room tied.

Still, I was getting the cold shoulder from the other players. I overheard Coach telling Kendra to "help Brittany along out there." I almost wished I was back on the bench and out of the spotlight.

We took the floor again for the second half. Sterling came out really hot, virtually unstoppable. Even with two of us on her, we couldn't contain her. "Come on Brit," Coach said. "Make a play. You can do it." His words inspired me, if only for the moment. Kendra rolled her eyes, but I was sure Coach was right. I could do something.

The next time Sherry had the ball, she tried to dribble by me. But I reached out and caught a piece of the leather. It rolled into Kendra's hands and she ran for an easy lay up. On the very next possession I stole the ball again. The excitement began to build. Yes, I was the shortest girl out there, and I didn't have the best shot either. But I could make things happen and I was showing everyone that. We scored another lay up and were in the lead.

I was feeling confident, so when Sherry dribbled toward me, I reached out again. This time, however, I didn't get the ball. Somehow, I lost my balance and went sprawling across the floor. I knocked both Kendra and Audrey to the ground. Sherry leaped over us, and scored easily. Everyone in the gym seemed to be laughing at us. Once again, I got dirty looks from Kendra and Audrey.

I dribbled up the court after my miscue and fired a pass into Kendra. But she missed an easy shot from three feet away. I'd seen her make a hundred of those short ones. We were so surprised she missed, that we didn't hustle back on defense. This gave Shenandoah an easy score on another fast break. They led by two now. We had to do something to keep the game close.

When Sherry drove the lane on the next play I

was in good position. My feet weren't moving, establishing that I was standing there before her. The ref would have to call a charging foul if she barreled me over.

Sure enough, I stood my ground and Sherry jumped into the air. She collided hard into my chest. The referee's whistle blew and I clapped my hands enthusiastically. But my ears couldn't believe what they heard. He was calling a blocking foul on me!

Right away, I ran over to him. "A foul?" I said, incredulous. "Are you blind? That's the worst call I've ever seen. She charged right over me!" I talked back to the ref, something Coach had warned us never to do. Just as I finished my yelling the whistle blew again. Technical foul.

My face turned red as Coach Holt called me to the bench. I took a seat far down, not daring to look at him. I was out of the game.

Although we still couldn't stop Sherry Sterling, Kendra got hot. We fed her the ball every trip down the floor. It was like magic. Kendra buried shot after shot. She managed to outplay the entire Shenendoah team.

We got the win, a close six-point victory. I should have been happy, but I was mortified. The other girls thought they'd won in spite of me. I showered and dressed quickly, attempting to leave the locker room before anyone else. Everyone pointedly ignored me. But before I could leave, Coach Holt called me into his office. I had no choice but to go in.

"Close the door, Brittany. Sit down." He sounded reasonably calm. "Want to tell me what happened out there?"

"I just lost it, Coach. I know we're not supposed to say anything to the refs. It just slipped out. I'm sorry." I looked down at my hands clenched into fists. "I know I didn't play well."

"You don't have a lot of game experience, but you played hard. I would have left you in. But after that technical, I had to send a message to the team. I don't tolerate that kind of thing."

I nodded, on the verge of tears.

His voice became quiet. "The girls gave you a hard time out there, huh?"

"Can't say that I blame them," I responded with a tear rolling down my cheek.

"It isn't easy breaking into a group that's played together. If you're not a hotshot, you're not readily accepted. And if you are a hotshot, everybody's jealous of you." He tossed me a bottle of water. "Basketball can be a tough game. Keep at it though. You'll find that balance."

I left his office and Eric was waiting for me outside. "Tough break," he said.

I must have looked really awful for Eric to be so nice to me. "Where's Brian?" I asked, hoping to change the subject.

"Begging Susan to take him back," he replied,

laughing.

"What'd he do?" The thought of Brian and Susan Ambler breaking up cheered me up.

"Nothing, she's just tired of him, I guess."

"So who's her new victim?" I didn't bother to hide my disgust.

Eric stumbled over the edge of the curb. "Don't know," he mumbled and started walking faster.

I didn't see much more playing time during the rest of the year. I got into some games late in the fourth when we were ahead by enough. The season went by quickly. Before I knew it, we were facing off against Shenandoah in our final game.

Shenandoah had a new gym with state-of-the-art loudspeakers and all sorts of fancy stuff. When the home team was announced, they put out all the lights and let each player run into a spotlight. I have to say, it was awesome. I wondered if I would ever get a chance to play in college, maybe have my name called in a spotlight.

Once the game started, Sherry Starling picked up where she'd left off in our gym. She swished nearly every shot she took. We plugged away the best we could but lost by fifteen points. Needless to say, the bus ride home was as silent as sleep.

CHAPTER FIVE

COACH JENSEN

Brian had recommended we take a ride in a cable car. So we did. It was so cool. The hills in San Francisco are amazing. And you can really see how steep they are from a cable car. We got off in San Francisco's Chinatown. "You still like Chinese food?" Brian asked.

"Still my favorite. I'm surprised you remembered."

Brian placed his hand on my back to steer me through a crowded street. This was a stronger and more experienced hand than I remembered from childhood. I admit, his touch gave me a thrill. I squinted up at him in the sun. I think he was a few inches taller now too.

We walked into a little restaurant with Chinese lanterns out front. "I used to come here all the time," Brian explained. "Sometimes we'd port in San Francisco for the night. This is where I'd have dinner." His stories were fascinating to me. He'd traveled all over the country— all over the world!

"You get to San Francisco often, then?" I inquired.

"My roommate at the Naval Academy was from here. We're both stationed at Bremerton, across Puget Sound from Seattle."

"So what are you going to do now that you're out of college?" He nodded toward my camera case. "Win the Pulitzer Prize?"

"Maybe," I grinned. "I definitely want to give photography a try. Unless——" My voice trailed off.

"Unless what?"

My heart beat a little faster as I confessed my dream. "I'd like to try to walk onto a WNBA team. Does that sound crazy?"

He got serious for a second. "No way, that sounds great."

I don't know if it was his easy smile or just the way he spoke, but I felt comfortable with Brian. He was exactly as I remembered him——and more. I poured us both a cup of tea. He spoke quietly, "I wonder what Eric would think of this."

"Think of what?" I asked.

He took a sip of tea. "Me and you, hanging out."

"Why would Eric care?" I was confused.

Brian laughed. "He wouldn't. Not now at least. It's just that—he used to give me such a hard time about you. Talk about an overprotective brother."

"Eric?" I asked.

"Oh yeah, he was impossible. I always wanted to ask you out during high school, but Eric was just too much." Did Brian just say that he always wanted to ask me out? This news was absolutely shocking to me. "I used to bug Eric all the time," Brian continued. "Eventually it was just a running joke. 'Hey, when you're not looking, I'm going to ask Brittany out.'"

I listened to him with my mouth wide open. I was in shock. My entire life, Brian had wanted to date me and Eric stood in his way. I'll kill him, I thought. But then a smile came to my face. Suddenly I wanted to call Eric and thank him for looking after me.

I looked over at Brian, "I don't know what to say." I paused. "I'm surprised to hear you say that." I wanted to tell him how I always loved him. I wanted to tell him that we should have been together this whole time. Instead, I blurted out, "Eric's not looking anymore."

I worked at the library to earn tuition money for basketball camp before junior year. I spent long hours putting books back into the right place on the shelves. Eric and Brian were life guards at the pool, basking in the sun. I spent my days reading every basketball book in that library. By August, I was itching to take my newfound knowledge onto the court. I had just turned sixteen when I headed to Tennessee for basketball camp. I couldn't have been more excited. Camps made a big difference in improving skills. And I knew that if I wanted to make varsity, I'd need to get much better.

The camp took place on a college campus in Knoxville, Tennessee. The summer heat nearly set me on fire when I stepped off the plane. My tour of campus was amazing. It was my first time on a college campus and I loved it. The library was enormous and the gym was even bigger. My final stop was the brand new aquatic center. Hundreds of kids were swimming and sunning in multiple swimming pools. If this was college, I couldn't wait.

For two weeks we ran drills and attended lectures on playmaking and proper fundamentals. And of course, we played lots of basketball. Every night, we were exhausted. We'd usually collapse into bed and fall asleep before nine o'clock. By the time camp was over, I knew I was a much better player. I also found out that I had reserves of strength and energy that I never even dreamed of.

On the plane ride back to D.C. I thought a lot about college. Where did I want to go? What did I want to study? These were tough questions that I didn't have answers to. I decided on one thing, though: When I did go to college, I was going to attend a smaller school than Tennessee.

When it came time for tryouts, the girl's varsity had a new coach. For me, this was not good news. Coach Holt would have seen my huge improvement and been very impressed. He would have definitely found a spot for me on varsity. But with a new coach, I had no idea what would happen. My game wasn't filled with flash. I wasn't sure how I would prove my value to her in a short tryout.

Coach Jensen introduced herself. She was young and pretty, with long blonde hair and a perfect smile. "There'll be a couple of new twists this year," she said in a soft voice. "For one thing, I'm holding the varsity and JV tryouts together." The upperclassmen groaned, while the freshmen and sophomores got excited. They'd now have a chance to make the varsity squad. Coach Jensen continued, "The rosters may also change. A player will not necessarily stay on the same team all season. There's room for improvement."

My first time on the court, I did OK. I got a few steals and made a couple of solid defensive plays. I focused on what I did best: playing defense and passing to the open player. I hoped this would be enough.

Tryouts passed quickly. I gave them all the effort I had. The good news was that the skills I had improved on during the summer definitely stood out. This was especially true of my ball handling. Unfortunately, Coach Jensen wouldn't post the results until

Monday.

Over the weekend, I was a nervous wreck. I tried to focus on other things but couldn't. I'd worked so hard—I just had to make varsity. I don't think I slept a wink Sunday night. I tossed and turned, wondering if my name would appear on the list.

At breakfast Monday morning, Eric sensed my nervousness. "You want me to check the list for you, Brit?" he offered.

"Do you mind?" I said at once, surprised by my brother's kindness. Then I took hold of myself. If I was too scared to look at the list, I was too scared to play on the team. "Actually, forget it. I guess I should look myself." I was trying to be brave.

"Even if you don't make the team, it's not the end of the world. Brian and I will still shoot hoops with you. We don't care if you're on varsity or not." I couldn't believe how nice he was being to me. Who was this guy? "You'll never be as good as us anyway, so don't worry about it." Now that sounded more like the Eric I knew.

I dismissed his comments and took a final bite of my pancakes before leaving. I had to get to school— to that list. When I approached the bulletin board, I got really nervous. I quickly scanned the names. "Ramirez, O'Connell, James, Washington, Conners, Ochoa, Price, Johnson, Heap. They had all been on the team before, so no surprise. I read on, "Andrews, Mayfield, Long, Chen, Smith, Short."

My eyes went back to the top of the list. I read it again and lowered my head. I didn't make it. A lump settled in my chest and stomach. It was so big I almost couldn't breathe. I guess I wasn't that surprised, but I'd worked so hard. If only Coach Holt were still here, I told myself, I would have made it.

As I turned to walk away, Marilyn called to me, "Brit, wait up." She hurried over. "So?" she said expectantly. "Are you going to play?"

"Obviously not," I said, trying to keep the bitterness out of my voice.

"No, I mean on junior varsity."

I just looked at her. I didn't have the foggiest idea what she was talking about.

"She put you, Kara, and Lisa on JV. They're in the math lab trying to decide what to do."

"JV?" My voice squeaked. I double checked the board. "Unbelievable," I whispered, "three juniors on JV?"

"And a freshman and two sophomores on varsity," she pointed out.

I raced over to the math lab. Kara and Lisa were there, and Lisa was dabbing at her eyes with a tissue. As bad as I felt, Lisa had taken an even bigger fall. She'd been a starter last season on JV and expected to make varsity without trouble. "That's it. I've had it!" She sobbed. "Nobody plays JV ball as a junior."

"I don't know how she can do this to us." Kara whined. "Well, she can't force me to play. Let her find somebody else. I quit."

"Me, too." Lisa added. She looked at me. "What about you, Brit?"

"I guess so." This was all happening too fast.

"Then let's go tell her," Kara said, dragging Lisa and me by the arm toward the gym.

"Wait, I can't——not now," I protested. "I have an English test first period."

"You chickening out?" Kara accused, her eyes burning with anger.

"I have a test. I'll tell her later." I shot Kara an annoyed look and left them, heading for English.

I went to see Coach Jensen just after last period. I wasn't sure what I was going to say to her exactly. I knocked on her half-open door. "Coach Jensen," I began.

She leaned back in her chair and regarded me skeptically. "Sit down."

Reluctantly, I did. When I started to speak, my heart nearly jumped out of my chest and into Coach Jensen's lap. "I——"

She grabbed a basketball and handed it to me. "Hold this, it'll relax you." I held the ball in my lap and suddenly felt a little less angry. "Feel a little better?" She spoke with a genuine kindness in her voice. Despite putting me on junior varsity, there was something really likable about Coach Jensen. "You're a junior, too, aren't you, Brittany? So I guess you're here to tell me you won't play on the JV team, either."

I rolled the ball around in my lap. "That's about the size of it," I conceded.

"Brittany, I know that I've ruffled some feathers here. I can assure you, I didn't mean to. I know that traditionally Junior varsity and varsity are divided. My high school operated that way too, and no one ever questioned it. But I think there's a better way. There are so many advantages to an open system, for the team and for the players."

"I don't see how it's an advantage for a junior to play on JV," I said.

"You're a playmaking point guard, Brittany," she said. "You need to play to refine your skills. Sitting on the bench is not a good way to develop. Frankly, you're not going to get the playing time on varsity this year. A season of playing, and I mean starting, will do wonders for you. I was a point guard just like you. I can help you get better. I see something special in you. That's why I did this."

I turned away but could feel her still looking at me. She was making a lot of sense. Playing and starting would do my game a lot of good. But still, there was one thought in my head overpowering the rest. I'm a junior, and juniors don't play JV.

I took a deep breath. "Maybe I should think about it."

She smiled and nodded. "That's great. Go home and sleep on it." She stood up. "You can let me know in the morning."

I nodded.

"And Brittany, think for yourself. Don't let your friends influence you. You have to do what's right for you."

I thought about this choice all the way home. Over dinner, I told Mom, Dad, and Eric about what Coach Jensen had said.

"It's not really quitting, you know," Eric said. "You didn't try out for the JV, you tried out for varsity."

"When I have a tough decision," Dad said, "I sit down with a piece of paper. I make a list of the advantages and a list of the disadvantages. Helps me to see things in black and white."

Later that night, I tried Dad's idea. On the good side, I would get to play basketball, and be a starter. On the bad side, there was some humiliation associated with being a junior on JV. When I was finished, there were five reasons I should play, four reasons I shouldn't. Not exactly an overwhelming victory for JV hoops. Still, I knew what I had to do. The next morning, I told Coach Jensen that I'd play for JV.

She smiled and reached out to shake my hand. "I don't think you'll be sorry. Lisa came by earlier and she'd like to play, too." My decision was suddenly looking a lot better. I wouldn't be the only junior on the team. I strolled off into the hallway and ran into Brian.

I told him what had just happened and he

seemed truly happy for me. Then he said something completely out of the blue. "That green shirt——it looks really good on you," he said. "It matches your eyes." I was speechless. You couldn't have convinced me he even knew what color my eyes were. Brian hesitated a minute. "Are you going to Marilyn's party Friday night?"

"Yes." I couldn't imagine why he was asking me that.

"Good. I'll see you there." He started to head into history class.

"Brian? You'll see me before then. Unless you guys are uninviting me to afternoon hoops today."

The normally unflappable Brian flushed a little pink. "Yeah, I mean no, that's not what I meant. You know, I'll see you at the party too."

That was weird, I thought. And a smile came to my face.

CHAPTER SIX

THINGS GET UGLY

A breeze began to blow in from the west and the fog crept overhead. "What time did you say your flight was?" Brian asked. We had just finished lunch and began a stroll along the bay.

"Six," I replied, snapping a photo of an extra-chubby seal by the water. "Our first team meeting starts at eight. Can't be late to that, the head coach is a stickler for time."

"Sounds like the military. Everyone's extra strict about time. You learn to adjust." Sometimes I forgot that Brian had been living a completely different kind of life during the past four years. The idea of being in the military was fascinating to me.

We walked for a minute before he stopped and looked at me with concern. "Are you sure you don't want to catch an earlier flight? I mean, I'm having a great time, but—"

"You're bored." I blurted out. Not the sort of thing Starling would have said.

"No, you could never bore me, Brit. Annoy, maybe, but bore?" We laughed and I took a picture of Brian. He tugged me along. "I was just thinking about the traffic. I mean, you're talking rush hour in Los Angeles, it could get pretty ugly."

"The meeting's at the team hotel, right by the airport. I'll be fine."

The wind blew a long strand of strawberry blonde hair across my face. Brian brushed it away with his hand. "It's so good to see you." He leaned in toward me and I felt the weight of the moment. Everything I'd thought about Brian and I had changed in the last hour. It turned out that he felt the same way about me that I felt about him back in high school. I hadn't spoken up because I was scared of what he would think. He hadn't confessed because he was scared of what Eric would think. Thoughts swirled through my head just before his lips touched mine. And then——HONK! A passing car quickly alerted us that we were in the middle of the street. I pulled away, startled. I moved back onto the sidewalk, following Brian's lead.

I soon realized that I'd made the right decision in playing JV ball. Not only was I a starter, the team even elected me as a captain. At first, the idea of leading the team frightened me. But after a few games, I realized that the point guard *should* be the leader. It made sense. So that was how I played. I was the coach on the floor, calling plays on the court. I monitored the game clock, the score, and the other team's defensive schemes. My teammates looked to me for direction. I tried to make sure everyone was on the same page. Coach Jensen said that when I was on the floor, her heart didn't beat quite as fast. I took that as a big compliment.

We had a freshman, Sandi Powers, who was a great player. She could score from anywhere on the court. This made my job a lot easier. I made sure that if she had an inch of open space, she had the ball. Unfortunately, like a lot of really good scorers, she was a ball hog. Once Sandi got the ball, she would rarely pass. I was a captain and a player two years her elder. Coach let me know that it was up to me to get her to change. I did it, too. By the end of that season, Sandi had changed. She learned to shoot when she was open, and pass when she was covered.

Coach Jensen told me that my leadership was my greatest accomplishment that year. She was particularly impressed with how I'd influenced Sandi. She said that this was something that never showed up on stat sheets and couldn't be taught. She also said that it was something every college coach looked for. College coach? Did she actually think I had a chance of playing in college? Relax, Brit, you have to make the varsity first.

I was feeling good about my game. I had accepted my role on the team. I wasn't going to be a superstar scorer. I was the leader on the floor. And I knew that this was every bit as important. On the plus side, my strength and endurance were coming along. And of course, I was nearly perfect with my foul shots.

Everything was going great until we played Madison High in our second to last game. We were tied with five minutes left in the fourth. I was bringing the ball up court but quickly drew the defense. Covered tightly, I passed it off to Sandi. She started to put it up, but realized I was open on the give-and-go. She made a bad pass back to me and my defender went after it. We both dove for the ball and collided. An instant later, the voice I heard screaming was my own.

Unfortunately, her finger, and expertly manicured nail, slashed into my right eyeball. I still shudder when I remember the scratchy, sharp pain.

Play was halted and both coaches took a look at me. My eye hurt so badly that I could hardly keep it opened. Eventually they determined that the injury wasn't too serious. Still, I had to sit out the rest of the game.

The next day my mom took me to an eye specialist. He insisted that I wear a pair of plastic goggles for the rest of the season. They looked like swimming goggles and even I had to laugh at myself. Eric and Brian got a lot of mileage out of my "visual appliance."

We finished the season with an impressive record of 14 and 5, winning our conference. While our season was over, the varsity team was in full swing. They finished third in their section, making them eligible for the district tournament. But just before the tournament, they lost two players to injury. Anita Ochoa tore a ligament in her knee and Roberta Johnson broke her pinky. Suddenly, there were two open roster spots on varsity.

Coach called me in and asked if I was ready for a new challenge. She wanted to put me on varsity. I was thrilled. Sandi moved up along with me, filling the other slot to Lisa's disappointment. I had finally made the varsity team. It was a great feeling of accomplishment.

Still, I did have to cope with being ignored by the rest of the team. I guess the girls felt that I didn't deserve to be there. Even Kendra acted as if we had never met. It was a good thing Sandi had moved up with me. Otherwise, I wouldn't have anyone to sit with on the team bus.

None of that mattered, though. I was on the Jefferson girls' varsity. I didn't mind that my jersey number was thirteen. I didn't mind that everyone claimed the number had jinxed Roberta, causing her to tear a ligament. And it didn't even matter that Mom and Coach insisted I continue wearing my "visual appliance." I was finally where I wanted to be. Well, almost. I was still on the bench.

Spring grades came out the day of the district semifinals. I did pretty well, all A's and B's. The discipline of practicing basketball taught me to stay organized and use my time wisely. Eric and Brian also did well. This was extra important for them because they were applying for college. Eric was good at math and science. But he wasn't sure what he wanted to do or where he wanted to go. Brian, however, had set his sights on the Naval Academy.

Getting word on spring grades wasn't such good news for one of my teammates. Michelle Conners got a terrible grade in English. Her report card had a big D on it. D for disaster, D for disqualified, D for dismissed. For Coach Jensen, any grade lower than a C meant you were benched. Coach relayed the tough message to us. She told us that Michelle was suspended and that I would start in her place.

"Don't worry, we're behind you, Brit," Coach said. I tried to believe her. But it was hard. As she spoke, dirty looks from my teammates darted my way one by one.

Before the game, during warm-ups, I was in a daze. I was starting on varsity in a critical road game against Shenandoah. I was also supposed to defend the player of the year, Sherry Sterling. She was beautiful, she was smart and she was as tough as they come.

I got over my butterflies as soon as the ball was tossed in the air for the opening tip-off. No time to worry now, I had to play my best. Overall, the first quarter went OK. I made a few mental errors, but we ended all tied up. Coach told us to slow things down and control the tempo. But it seemed that every time Sherry Sterling touched the ball, she scored. Fortunately for us, Kendra was just as hot. We went into the locker room at the half trailing by only four.

In the third quarter, we battled back to a tie. I was doing okay, holding my own with a steal here and there. But never, I admit, off of Sterling. Then things got ugly. The avalanche began on a routine play. I was bringing the ball up-court when Sherry whizzed by me so fast I didn't even see her. The next thing I knew, I was running toward our basket without the ball. Sterling had stolen it from me, taking it the other way for a lay up. I couldn't believe it. The ball had only been stolen from me twice all year.

On the very next play, Sherry did it again. She stole the ball from me and scored another easy basket. And it got worse. The following inbounds pass went right through my fingers as if they were greased. Sterling grabbed the loose ball and made another jumper. This one was from the foul line. Mercifully, Coach Jensen called a time-out to calm me down. Everyone on our team shot the "evil eye" at me.

After the timeout, I brought the ball up slowly and deliberately. We were down by ten. Kendra came out to meet me and I passed the ball safely to her. As a team, we were playing too cautiously. Finally, Kendra tossed it to me as the shot clock went down to three. "Take it, Brit!" she shouted. When I didn't move immediately, she shouted at me again. "Put it up!"

I obeyed and promptly launched an air ball. I wanted to disappear, vanish into thin air. But instead, the ball found its way back to me again. I was back in the spotlight. Sterling saw that I was shaken and reached for another steal. Luckily, the ref called a foul this time.

I stepped up to the free-throw line, completely rattled. I took a deep breath. At least I can redeem myself here, I thought. I put up the ball the way I always do. But this one hit the front of the rim——not even close. Kendra looked at me and shook her head. My hands started to shake as I prepared for the second shot. Concentrate, Brittany. Clank, off the side of the rim this time. As if she hadn't done enough damage, Sterling grabbed the rebound and went down the court for another lay up.

Coach Jensen signaled for another time-out. When I got to the sidelines I had tears in my eyes. "You're a bundle of nerves, Brittany," she said. "Have a seat and calm down." I slunk off and sank down on the end of the bench. "Sandi!" Coach yelled briskly. "Take Kendra's position at forward. And Kendra, you bring the ball up. Come on, let's get back into this thing."

Sandi didn't have to be told twice. She came in and never looked back, firing up one shot after another. She scored thirteen points in the fourth quarter alone. We managed to hold on for a two-point victory. I didn't play another minute of that game.

With only one day of practice before the big game, everyone was tense and edgy. Kendra was constantly asking for Sandi to replace me in the lineup. But when Coach Jensen began practice, she started me at point guard again. That was a really tough practice. Coach had everybody coming at me, trying to rattle me. That was just fine by me. I never wanted to be publicly humiliated in a game again.

But my teammates weren't convinced I could do it. On the day of the game, I was sitting in the school cafeteria alone. All of a sudden, Kendra and two other seniors sat down at the table beside me. "About tonight," Kendra began, looking at the other girls and than at me. "We don't think you should play."

I looked up in total surprise.

Chris and Liz nodded. "You can tell Coach you're sick," Liz urged. "It happens all the time."

"You saw for yourself the other night," Chris chimed in. "We're much better with Kendra at point guard and Sandi playing forward."

I knew they had doubts about me, but I had no idea they felt this strongly. My mouth must have hung open. I couldn't think of a thing to say.

"Just say that you don't feel well," Kendra said. "Or tell her you're scared. We don't really care what you say, as long as you don't play. You want the team to win, don't you?"

I didn't answer. They walked away, leaving me there alone. It was the worst I'd felt in my entire life. I looked up to see Brian standing over me. "I heard that," he said.

I swallowed hard, trying to hide how much they had hurt me.

"You're not going to let them frighten you off, are you?" His blue eyes had a hard, determined edge.

I stared off into space, biting my lip to keep from crying.

"You're stronger than that, Brit."

Brian was right. I stood up, stuck my chin out, and spoke with a newfound confidence. "You're right. I'm way stronger than that." I got up and gave Brian a hug, probably the first one we'd ever shared. Eventually, I let go. But I could have stayed in his arms forever.

My last class of the day was world history, and it ran a little late. I had to hustle. Racing to the locker room, I threw my gear into my red bag. When I got outside, most of the team had already boarded the bus. The rest of the players were waiting for Coach Jensen, who was in her office on the phone. Everyone ignored me and I ignored them. I walked down the aisle and tossed my bag up with the others in the back of the bus. "I'm playing," I announced to no one in particular, finding a seat up front.

The bus ride was much quieter than usual. We

were extra focused for the big game. When we arrived, we all grabbed our gear, rushed off the bus, and headed for the locker rooms.

But I couldn't find my gym bag with the others in the back of the bus. I raced to the locker room, figuring someone must have brought it in by mistake. I glanced around, hoping to see it right away. There were all different bags tossed in every direction around the locker room. I looked through them and had no luck. My bag was dark red and the zipper was broken——and it was definitely missing. I stalked around asking if anyone had seen my bag.

"Brittany, get a move on," Coach Jensen shouted. Everyone else was already getting into uniform.

I was in a panic. Tears were beginning to form in my eyes. I tore through piles of clothes, my heart racing. Everyone else had dressed and was out of the locker room. Still no gym bag. I slumped down on the cold, hard floor, unable to believe what was happening.

"Brittany?" Coach Jensen stormed into the locker room again.

"My bag's missing. I loaded it on myself," I said, tears raining down my face. "They didn't want me to play, they hid it."

She came over and knelt down beside me. "Let's hope there's another explanation, Brit." She patted me on the shoulder and shuffled through some loose clothes, "I'm so sorry this happened to you. When we find out who did this, they're in a lot of trouble. But you know I can't let you out there without your protective glasses."

"I know," I managed to choke.

She stood up. "The game's about to start. Come on out and sit on the bench with us."

I managed to pull myself together and went out there. My eyes were so puffy I could hardly see out of them. Somehow I made it through the game without crying again. I was relieved when it finally ended. We won in overtime, but I was too miserable to care. Eric was nice enough to give me a ride home. The last thing I wanted was to get back on the bus with the team. I went to bed heartsick that night.

The next day, Mom gave us a ride to school. I begged her to let me stay home so I didn't have to face anyone. But as she said, "You have to go back sometime. The longer you stay away, the worse it'll be."

Actually, it wasn't that bad at all. Several of my classmates heard what happened and were sympathetic. Coach Jensen called me in and asked me exactly what the girls had said to me at lunch. Three days later, my missing gym bag was found in the back of a supply closet. When Coach questioned Kendra, Chris, and Liz, she found out everything she needed to know. They left her office suspended from the first game of the regional tournament.

I was eligible and I started. I don't think you'll be surprised to learn that we lost. South Roanoke was a great team and two of our starters were ineligible. Maybe we would have lost anyway, but we'll never know. Did the bag controversy make me even more unpopular with my teammates? With some, probably. But most of them recognized that what happened wasn't my fault.

CHAPTER SEVEN

SHERRY STERLING

"The parking garage is over there," I said, pointing to a blue neon sign that read PARK. Just as we started walking, a plane roared across the sky above us. Immediately, Brian jerked his head up.

I had to laugh. "You haven't changed a bit. Still distracted by anything that flies, huh?"

He grinned sheepishly. I followed his gaze and noticed a tall, triangularly shaped building. "What's that?" I asked.

"Oh, that's the Transamerica Pyramid. It's the tallest building in San Francisco. Great views from the top."

I glanced at my watch, then up at the building. "I think we have some time. You wanna go up?"

Brian grinned at me. "I thought you were

afraid of heights." He reached out to touch a strand of my hair. "Whatever happened to the skinny little girl with freckles and braces?" There was a moment of silence and I'm sure I blushed. Brian grabbed my hand. "So you wanna go up?"

A moment later we were in the lobby. We got in a line for the elevator that led to the observation deck. "You think you have time?" Brian asked, as we inched forward slowly.

I checked my watch again. "It's worth seeing, right?" I ventured.

"Best sight in the city," he acknowledged, "and the elevators are fast too."

"Then don't sweat it." I was really torn now. I couldn't miss my flight to Los Angeles. My watch read 3:39 and my flight was scheduled to depart at 6:00. Assuming we'd board at 5:30, I had less than two hours to see the top of this building, make it all the way down, get the rental car, navigate through traffic to the airport, get my bag, check in, and board the plane before takeoff. I knew I was cutting things very close. But I just couldn't tear myself away from Brian.

"The Olympics are in Seattle this year, aren't they?" he asked.

"Yup, the Emerald City," I replied.

"If you make the team, I'll fly over the stadium with your name on a banner."

"Don't say that," I warned. "You'll jinx me."

"Still superstitious?" he teased, as we finally stepped onto the crowded elevator.

"I think I'm more superstitious than ever. You know I still have the Washington state quarter you gave me for good luck the first time I ever tried out for a team. I won't go anywhere without it. And now I'm trying out for the Olympics——in Washington. Pretty weird, huh?" As soon as these words had left my mouth, I wanted to take them back. He probably didn't even remember giving me that quarter. He wasn't going to see the coincidence!

"You still have that quarter?" His voice rose and the dimple in his cheek was more wildly attractive than ever.

"I keep it in my shoe," I blushed slightly. *"That's why I've been so lucky."*

"I gave that to you when I coached the team you tried out with. I remember that." He continued, jokingly, *" I was the one who put you at point guard. Maybe I should be coaching the Olympic team."*

The elevator stopped and we got out. We walked a few feet to the edge of the observation deck. *"What'd I tell you?"* Brian said as we looked out across the bay. *"Isn't this something?"*

I saw the fog rolling in over the Golden Gate Bridge. *"It's beautiful,"* I was totally floored. *"So what's better, this or the view from the cockpit?"*

Brian smiled. *"It's pretty close, but I'd have to give it to the cockpit."* He put his arm casually around *my shoulder, pointing toward an island in the middle of the bay. "That's Treasure Island. I spent a couple of months training there."*

"Flying?" I managed to squawk. His nearness was robbing me of my voice as well as my wits.

"No, I did flight school in Florida, and training on the F-16 in San Diego."

"You sure get around, Brian." Another brainless comment. Get a grip, Brittany.

He laughed and turned to look at me, his back to the windows. "Where's your camera? We can get someone to take a picture of the two of us. Maybe we can send it to Eric. He'd get a kick out of it."

I was in such a daze that I let my camera slide right through my fingers. It landed on the deck. We both knelt down to pick it up. Our hands closed over the camera at the same time. My heart started to race in my chest. I looked up to see Brian's eyes staring into mine. He reached out to me, his finger straying across the base of my chin. I closed my eyes as he leaned in to kiss me. We were both still kneeling on the ground to pick up the forgotten camera. I'd waited for that kiss for what seemed like forever.

Prom was a disaster. I got to go during my junior year, which was kind of a tradition in my high school. All the senior guys took junior girls. You can imagine my pain when I found out that Brian had asked Sherry Sterling. Eric, filled me in on every detail from the corsage to the color of Sherry's dress.

Marc Iaccone was my date. He was tall, about six-foot-five, and had this habit of saying everything twice. When he came up to me at my locker and said, "Hey Brit, we're sharing a limo with Brian and Eric, we're sharing a limo with Brian and Eric," I knew I was in trouble. Picture this: an hour-long limousine ride with me wedged between Susan Ambler and Sherry Sterling! It was a nightmare.

I don't think I said a word the entire ride. I tried to avoid making eye contact with Brian, Susan, Sherry, and especially my date, Marc. "This limo's huge, this limo's huge," Marc whispered to me just as we arrived. Not huge enough, I thought.

Six months later, the prom disaster was in the rearview mirror. I was a senior at Jefferson and on top of the world. Eric had settled on Richmond Tech and Brian went off to the Naval Academy. That winter, I approached varsity basketball tryouts with more confidence. I returned to the camp at Tennessee College that summer and made major improvements. When I got back home, something happened for me on the basketball court. I was twice the player I had been a year earlier. Plus, I'd grown a lot from the painful experience of having my teammates hide my gym bag.

Kendra turned out to be OK. She must have apologized a thousand times. She even bought me a new bag as a gesture of friendship. That entire fall, she, Lisa, and I practiced relentlessly. We all made the team easily and the starting lineup, along with Sandi and Beth Silver.

We were determined to make the most of our final year in high school. I had developed a good jump shot to go along with my passing and game management skills. Plus, I hardly ever turned the ball over. My stat line usually looked something like this: eight points, ten assists, three or four steals, a few rebounds, and no turnovers.

By mid-season, we were undefeated. College scouts appeared at our games and Kendra got dozens of letters from them. She got attention from colleges we'd never even heard of. I was a little jealous, but I was also realistic. With few basketball scholarships available, they were reserved for only the best.

Nothing about my game set me apart from everyone else. I would approach scouts and they would point out reasons they were passing me over. Some said I was too short. Others said I needed work on shooting off the dribble. I did get complimented several times on being a good defender. But these compliments would be followed by more criticism. Many scouts were concerned I wouldn't be able to defend bigger guards in college. They also didn't think a person of my size would rebound well.

"You've got a great big heart in a real small body," one scout said. "Any team that offered you a scholarship would be going out on a limb." Although comments like these discouraged me, I didn't give up. I wrote letters and sent tapes to every major basketball program in the country. Unfortunately, I never got one response. But I would still try to walk onto a basketball team somewhere.

Though I wouldn't get a basketball scholarship, there was some good news. My SAT scores were great, even better than Eric's had been. Naturally, I didn't waste any time calling to let him know. I also had excellent grades, so I knew I could get into a good college. I was looking for a small school. It needed to have a good fine arts program and a basketball team that I could try to walk on. But my senior season was going to be a huge factor in this decision.

Luckily, that season was by far our most successful. We clicked. There is no other way to say it. When we stepped onto the floor we were a unit. We played together like a band playing a piece of music to perfection. We won our conference with ease, and thus earned an automatic bid into the second round.

Once again, Sherry Sterling stood in our way. Our rivalry was heightened after my brother told me she had visited Brian at Annapolis. I supposed this meant that she was dating Brian. This made me crazy. Now she was getting to me off the court as well as on. I couldn't wait for my chance to beat her in a game.

Both teams came out excited, and played completely out of control early on. By the end of the first quarter, Lisa and I had two fouls each. The game was tied at sixteen and the big shooters on both teams were hot. I had two points on a jump shot that I took right over the top of Sterling. I have to say it felt extra good to score on her. But I knew my responsibility was to get the ball to Kendra and Sandi. I couldn't get into a shooting contest with Sterling. If I did, we would lose for sure.

Since hitting that jumper, Sterling started coming out further to defend me. This opened up the passing lanes, helping me to seven assists in the first quarter.

We went into the locker room at halftime, clinging to a two-point lead. Everyone was huffing and puffing and not really speaking to one another. Coach Jenson sensed our physical and emotional exhaustion right away. She started clapping her hands and turned the faucets on at the sinks. She told us to place our heads under the faucet for a few seconds. Not only was this refreshing, but funny as well. We all began laughing when the cold water hit our heads. The mood lightened almost immediately.

We came out more relaxed for the third quarter. But still, we were very much aware of our slim two-point lead. I brought the ball up-court and found Kendra. She split the defenders in the lane, and drove right to the basket. She laid it in exactly as we'd drawn it up in the locker room. Up by four.

I was itching for a steal on the next possession. Sterling dribbled by me and I reached out, tipping the ball as she passed. Sandi grabbed it and raced for an easy lay up. Sterling shot a fiery look my way. I glanced up at the scoreboard; we were up 46 to 40. Coach Jensen held up a clenched fist, which meant a full-court press. She was hoping to build on our lead by creating turnovers.

I pestered the Shenandoah guard trying to in-bound the ball. I jumped, flailed my arms and was just a complete nuisance. She couldn't get the ball past half-court and had to call time-out.

"Good," I shouted to nobody in particular. I was clapping my hands and looking right at Sterling. "Let's use up those timeouts!" My outburst surprised even me. I was usually pretty quiet on the court. But when I looked at Sherry, I thought of her and Brian. It made me want to scream.

But the game wasn't over yet. On the inbounds pass they caught us flat-footed. Sterling made a shot and Sandi fouled her in the process. Naturally, Sterling made it a three-point play and, now, a three-point game. But this was a war for me, and it was very personal. I came right back down and buried a three-pointer over her outstretched hands. With seven seconds left in the quarter, we were up by six. I stared over at Sterling again. Sure enough, on the next play she answered me right back. As the buzzer sounded, she threw up a prayer from half-court. Somehow, it slammed off the backboard and into the hoop. So at the end of the third quarter, we led 50 to 47.

The fourth quarter started out like a wrestling match. It was brutal. Each trip down the floor,

Shenendoah would pound the ball inside. After establishing their scoring near the basket, they began zeroing in on Sandi. They knew she was our youngest starter, and they thought they could rattle her. They were right. They made sure that whomever Sandi was guarding defensively would get the ball. And every time Sandi touched the ball, they'd scream, "Shoot! Shoot!" They put the entire game on her shoulders and she folded like a newspaper. The pressure was too much for Sandi. She lost her focus, throwing the ball away three times in a row. After five minutes of this Sandi was near tears.

Coach was forced to pull her from the game just to calm her down. Shenandoah was up by one, and Sterling brought up the ball. I got in position in front of her and she finally got called for charging. Her eyes flashed at me in anger, and she said something under her breath. I didn't quite catch it, but I knew she wasn't wishing me luck. I stared into her eyes. In those moments, it felt like she and I were the only two people in the building.

During a pause in the action, I looked over at the crowd. I noticed a man sitting with about ten small children around him. They held up signs with Sherry's name on it. I figured it must be her family. I wondered how Sherry could belong to such a nice family. It just didn't seem to fit. Her dad was wiping ice cream from his son's face while keeping watch over the rest. Where's her mother, I thought. But my attention went back to the game when I heard the ref's whistle. Beth Silver inbounded the ball to me and I dribbled down the court. I launched a quick shot that missed, but Sterling had fouled me in the process. I made the first free-throw with ease. Then I took a deep breath and put the other one up. It ricocheted around the rim forever, but finally dropped. I sighed with relief. We now led by one with two minutes to play.

Andee Kim took the ball for Shenandoah. Lisa and I closed in to cut off the path to Sterling. If they were going to beat us, someone else would have to make a shot.

That's when I felt it first, a sharp tug on my hair. It was so sudden and so strong, that it snapped my neck back. I thought I saw Sterling's hand leave my hair as she received a pass. She put it up and in before I could make another move. Somehow the refs let her get away with an obvious foul.

Shenandoah went ahead by one.

I inbounded the ball to Sandi, over the heads of two Shenendoah players. She then passed it over to Kendra, who passed it back to me. I put it up from the top of the key. I knew that it was in right when I released it. Swish! I looked over at Sterling again.

Thirty seconds left. We led by one, 66 to 65. I had scored eighteen points, tying my season high. Andee dribbled past half-court, looking frantically for Sterling to get open. The next thing we knew, Sterling was screaming. The whistle sounded and the referee pointed to Lisa. She started to say something to the official, but thought better of it. Lisa had fouled out and had to leave the game. This gave Sterling two free-throw attempts with just six seconds to go.

She sank the first one, tying the game. She set herself and put up the next one. This one was off target. It bounced off the rim, and we all rushed into the paint. A dozen grabbing, scratching, clawing hands fought to catch it.

Somewhere near the pack of sweaty, slick bodies, the ball came to me. Just as my fingers closed on it, something hit me hard in the stomach. The wind was knocked out of me and I dropped the ball. A second later, I heard a tremendous roar and then the sound of the buzzer.

When I looked up from the bottom of the pile, the game was over.

I learned later that Sterling had charged the pile like a football player. She practically vaulted over everyone to score the winning basket. We lost by two points, and our season was over. For us seniors, our careers at Jefferson were too.

After the game, I thought a lot about college next year. I wondered if I would be able to walk onto a team. I thought about getting another shot at Sterling too. But more than anything, I thought about the possibility that I had just played the last game of my basketball career.

CHAPTER EIGHT

NORTHERN VIRGINIA

After about twenty minutes on the observation deck, Brian and I were ready to head back down. We needed to hustle to get to the airport in time for my flight. But a security guard was standing in front of the elevators. "I don't know if you folks felt it, but we just had a slight earthquake. Nothing to worry about, but the elevators will be down for an hour or so. Just a precaution." I couldn't believe it. I was going to miss my flight. The man continued, "If you're in a hurry the staircase is to your left." There was only one choice——forty-three flights of stairs.

After running down twenty floors, Brian and I were completely out of breath. "We better start walking or we're not going to make it," he said.

Our pace slowed to a quick walk. "What time

is it, Brian?" I panted. I was beginning to get really nervous.

"Four fifteen," Brian confessed. "Hey, at least we're climbing down and not up." He was much calmer than I was. But then again, he didn't have a 6:00 plane to catch.

Out of breath, we stumbled onto the city streets from the stairwell. "Uh oh," Brian moaned. "Looks like the traffic lights are out too." And that wasn't even the worst of it. The city streets were in a gridlock. Horns were honking, lights were flashing, and my heart was pounding. All my work, all my dreams were vanishing right in front of me. How could I be so stupid?

"I'm getting really worried, Brian," I said with tears welling in my eyes.

"We'll make it," he said, putting his hand on my back.

We turned into the parking garage. "No more stairs," I pleaded.

"We're only parked on the third level. Want a piggyback?" he offered.

"If it's more than three flights, I might take you up on it."

Nine months after the game against Shenandoah, I arrived at Northern Virginia University. I was an eighteen-year-old college freshman. After just a few weeks, I knew I'd made the right choice by coming to UNV. My classes were great and I'd already made a bunch of close friends.

I spent most of my spare time honing my skills for basketball tryouts. The day of tryouts was a dismal, rainy fall afternoon. The bad weather matched the depressing outlook for the day. There were seventeen of us competing for just two positions. The other twelve spots on the team had already been filled with scholarship players. All seventeen of us had been good, if not great players in high school. And as usual, I was the smallest one on the court.

What was even worse, though, was that today was the only day of tryouts. That meant I had only one chance to impress Coach Fleming. Each time I passed him I walked on my tip-toes. Sometimes, I would take a deep breath to make myself look bigger. I don't think I was fooling anyone.

Sixteen of the girls trying out were freshman. Only one of us, Rosa Santos, was a sophomore. I could see right away that she would be the toughest to beat out. She was a transfer student with a year of college basketball under her belt. Rosa was tough and scrappy with a great three-point shot. She would make the team, no question about that. Whichever player stood out the most would join her. I knew I had to play my very best to be that player.

Coach Fleming matched us up for some three-on-three games. We did this for three straight hours! I played well throughout, but in the last game, I put on a real show. I finished with three steals, a blocked shot and four rebounds. That's right, I got four rebounds! And on offence, I was nothing short of spectacular. I scored all eleven of my team's points and hadn't missed a shot.

"OK, girls," Coach Fleming yelled, blowing his whistle. "That's it."

We trooped off the court and collapsed on the benches. He came over and tossed a ball to Rosa. "You all put up a good fight. So thanks for coming out." This was a much different tryout than any other I had been to. Mainly because nobody that was there except Rosa, expected to make the team. After all, most of the roster was made up of scholarship players. Coach Fleming knew this and was quick and matter-of-fact when he said, "Rosa Santos, and Brittany Bristol, I'll see you two tomorrow afternoon for practice."

I had played my very best and I had stood out from the rest. Brittany Bristol was on a college basketball team! How about that? I made sure to call almost everyone I knew that night to share the news. Overall, I think people were pretty shocked. Everyone in my life had been rooting for me, but I don't think anyone, besides Mom and Dad, truly believed I was going to do it. The surprise I heard in their voices added to my feeling of accomplishment. I'd done something no one, including myself, expected me to do.

When the season opened a month later, I was

just happy to be there. As a freshman walk-on, I knew my playing time would be limited. I was the third string point guard behind two seniors. So I kept a pretty low profile, just trying to learn the system. I also tried to navigate my way through the difficulties in the locker room. And in our locker room that year, it was extremely difficult.

The trouble started because of the situation with Clarissa. She took the starting position of a popular senior from the year before. The other seniors thought this was an injustice, and pointed their anger directly at Clarissa. And that was only the beginning of the trouble.

The upperclassmen even refused to pass the ball to Clarissa. Coach Fleming pleaded with them, but nothing he said made any difference. He had lost total control of his team. To be honest, Clarissa didn't make things any easier on herself.

"I'm headed to the dining hall," I said one day after practice. I looked over at Clarissa. "Do you want to come?"

"I'm busy," she mumbled, grabbing her bag and racing out of the locker room.

"Miss Personality," mocked Roz Smythe, the senior who'd lost her starting position to Clarissa.

"You got that right," twittered Amy Ross and Reina Klein, the other starting seniors.

All the senior girls were very close, since three started and the other two were our top subs. But their heads were in another place altogether. They certainly didn't seem to care much about basketball. Rosa was convinced it was because the team had never been very good and they simply had no pride.

But the senior clique was only one problem. Kelly Washington, our junior center, was tight with the other two juniors on the team. They went everywhere together and rarely spoke to the rest of us. So there was yet another exclusive clique. Plus, the two sophomores, Kayla O'Grady and Aziz Khan, disliked Rosa. When Rosa made the team, she replaced the player who didn't make grades—Kayla's twin sister, Karla.

Then there were us freshmen. We weren't really a clique; we were kind of just there. Besides Clarissa and me, there was Ming Kuo, a Chinese girl from New York City who spoke very little English, and Andrea Summers, a beauty queen from a small town in North Carolina. I was convinced the only reason Andrea played basketball was to be seen. She had a wicked jumper, though.

Considering all our cliques, it was no surprise that we were dead last in our conference. To makes things worse, nobody—and I mean nobody—came to our games. Morale was very low, and Clarissa was struggling in each game. She had come into the season as the top high school basketball player in the country. She was supposed to be a star. I could tell she was really down, even though she never said anything. But you can't score if no one ever passes you the ball!

One evening in late January, I missed my history notebook and remembered I'd last seen it in the locker room. I hurried back across campus. It was dusk and just beginning to snow. Hamilton Gym was almost dark, but a few lights were still on. I let myself in. Just as I touched the door to the locker room, I could hear someone sobbing softly. Now, I didn't want to intrude, but I had a history test the next morning. I had to go in and get my notebook.

I eased the door open and stepped in quietly. Right away I saw my notebook on the bench near the shower area. I knew someone was in there, but I didn't see a soul. I tiptoed across the room. Just as my hand landed on the face of my notebook, I saw Clarissa. She was sitting on a bench, hunched over, hugging her knees and crying.

"Clarissa? What's wrong?" I could hardly go away and pretend I didn't see her. She looked up at me, tears streaming down her face. "Why are you crying?" I asked.

She shook her head. "Just go away," she hissed. Her voice was hard and angry.

I felt bad for her. I sat down beside her and reached over to touch her shoulder. "What is it?" I asked.

She started to jerk away, but then gave up and started wailing. "I hate it here!" she sobbed. "I want to go home."

"Everybody feels like that sometimes." I rubbed her shoulder. "Did something happen?"

"No," she spat out through tears and sniffles, "just the same old thing. Everybody hates me. Nobody likes me."

"Nobody hates you," I insisted. "Nobody really knows you."

"They all want me out of here," she continued. "They don't even let me touch the stupid ball."

I sighed. How could I argue with that? "They're just jealous."

"Teammates aren't supposed to be jealous," she choked out.

"You're right. But this team isn't like any I've ever played on." I thought for a while. "How about you?"

She shook her head.

"Well, maybe we can turn it around," I suggested. Truthfully though, I didn't have the slightest idea how.

Clarissa raised her head and looked at me with her watery eyes. "You and me?"

What was I getting us into? "We could try," I replied, with more conviction than I felt.

Clarissa fumbled in her pocket for a tissue. "Problem with me is," she said, "it's hard for me to get to know people."

"You're just shy," I said.

"I hear what they call me. Miss Personality,"

she snorted.

"Don't let them bother you," I scolded. "It's tough being the new girl. But next year, five seniors are graduating. Everything will change then. You just have to stick it out."

"But what can we do about it right now?" she asked.

"I don't know," I said, honestly. "Maybe take them out to dinner."

Clarissa began to brighten up. "What if we made cookies and invited the girls over to our floor——"

I started to like this idea. "——on like a Sunday night, when we don't have practice," I chimed in.

"——and maybe we can get to know each other."

"——and talk." I thought a minute. This wasn't such a bad idea.

The following Sunday afternoon, Clarissa and I were busy in the kitchen. We studied for our English exam while chocolate chip cookies baked in the oven. I'm a total loss in the kitchen, but Clarissa really knew how to cook. She said her grandmother taught her.

Ming and Andrea, the other two freshmen, came over to help us. We invited the rest of the team over, too, but only Rosa came. For the rest of the season, we continued our Sunday night get-togethers. Those of us who came grew closer. We freshmen were always there, even if Andrea had to pass up a date. Rosa also came, and sometimes one or two of the juniors came, too.

We finished the season in second to last place in our conference. When Coach Fleming announced his retirement, we were all buzzing about who might replace him. With seven players leaving, we'd have a whole new look next year. For us freshman, it couldn't have been more exciting. Next season, as sophomores, we would be a critical part of the team.

CHAPTER NINE

SOPHOMORE YEAR

We finally made it to the car on the third floor of the parking garage. When Brian turned the engine on, my eyes went immediately to the digital clock on the dashboard. "Four twenty-four."

We zipped down the ramps and headed for the exit. We then quickly turned the corner to exit the garage. Then Brian slammed his fist against the steering wheel. There was a line of cars in front of us at the cashier's booth. What was worse was that it appeared that the gate was stuck closed. With the electricity out, there was no way to open it. We were all stuck. Horns were honking all around us. Brian jumped out of the car, approaching the booth.

A tall man with a grizzly beard spoke helplessly as Brian approached him, "Power's out and the bar won't go up."

"You've got to be kidding," Brian said.

*"I wish I was, but there's nothing I can do."
The man shrugged his shoulders and took a sip from
a can of soda. I put my head in my hands. I was
frustrated that I was going to be cut from the team
before I'd even been given a chance. Sherry Sterling
was probably having dinner with the coaching staff
right now. I was stuck behind six cars in a parking
garage.*

*All around us, people were starting to panic
along with me. The cashier came out of the booth.
He took a look at the gate bar that was stuck in the
down position. Brian spoke over his shoulder and
the man nodded his head again and again. Finally
I heard the man say, "You can try."*

*Brian stood in front of the gate and shouted to
the line of cars, "Does anyone have a screwdriver?"*

*Immediately, one guy popped open his trunk
and started looking around. "I got one." He held up
a mini screwdriver and tossed it to Brian.*

*A second later, Brian was bending over the
bar. I jumped out to help him. He began unscrewing
it from the hinges. I got down on my knees and un-
screwed the bolts as soon as Brian had loosened them.
In only a few minutes, Brian was able to lift the heavy
bar aside. He stood and shouted to the crowd, "OK,
pay up and get out."*

The crowd cheered as Brian took a quick bow

and we rushed back to the car.

"See, Brit," he said, as he turned the igni-tion, "we make a great team."

"That was awesome." I smiled. There was still a chance I could make my flight.

The summer before my sophomore year was again devoted to basketball. I was a counselor at a basketball day camp back home in Oak Grove. I got to play basketball every single day. Eric was home for the summer too, working at a local vet's office. I saw him all the time and we even played some one-on-one games. I'm happy to say that I won them all. We didn't see Brian though, because he was on a summer cruise with the Navy. As usual, before I knew what happened, summer was over.

Sophomore year at UNV got off to a great start. Our new coach was Dana Hollins, and she brought in two junior college transfers. They were good players that jumped right into our starting lineup at point guard and forward. Kelly, our returning center, was now a senior. Clarissa continued at power forward and Rosa won the shooting guard spot. I moved up to the backup point guard position. Coach Hollins offered me a full scholarship for the next three years at UNV. A free college education! Mom and Dad were thrilled.

We continued our Sunday evening cookie par-ties. With none of the cliques from the year before, everyone started showing up. The team really began to gel together. We were still different personalities, but we were learning a lot about one another.

Clarissa was more at ease now too. She was getting along with most of the girls and our friendship was blossoming. Ming really came out of her shell in the informal atmosphere of the dorm kitchen get-togethers. She introduced us to a bunch of delicious and exotic Chinese desserts. By the end of sophomore year, she was speaking English like she'd been born here. And Andrea had traded in boys for basketball. Well, some boys.

I didn't get much playing time during my sophomore year. Still, I considered it a successful season. I played about six minutes a game and improved dramatically. Just being out there in pressure situations was great experience for me. As a team, we improved over last season. Clarissa was our leading scorer, and she led the conference in rebounding too.

Our strong regular season earned us a trip to the NCAA tournament. That was good news. But when we won our first round game, we were in uncharted territory. We became the first team in school history to get past the first round of the tournament. Our second round opponent was Southern Maryland. This was bad news for us. They were big, athletic, and mean looking. The Crabs were ranked seventh in the entire nation. Winning this game would be a small miracle.

As it turned out, we played the best game of our season that day. With eight minutes left, we were only down by two points. It was then that Kirsten, our starting point guard, fouled out.

"Brittany!" Coach Hollins screamed. "Eight minutes left, this is your team now." A chill ran down my spine. I checked into the game with more excitement than ever before. I would be playing the biggest game of my life, and on national television.

I brought the ball up-court deliberately, determined to control the pace. Right away, Nikki Cruz, the top Crab, lunged for a steal. I wasn't going to let that happen. I slung the ball behind my back to Rosa, who put a up a three. Swish! We now led by one. The excitement in the arena was starting to build.

Southern Maryland answered us immediately with a jump shot from the corner.

I dribbled up-court again, looking for Kelly inside. She wove her way under the basket and back out. I glanced in Rosa's direction and then faked a pass to Clarissa. Cruz went for the fake. This gave me a passing lane up above the defense. So I quickly arched the ball over to Kelly. She had come back under the basket, and tapped it in. A whistle sounded. Foul on Southern!

Kelly came to the line with us leading, 56 to 55. She fired. Bottom! 57 to 55. We had a two point lead with less than two minutes to play. I was controlling the game. I was playing like a confident leader. And I was moving the ball around to my teammates in positions for them to score. This was the definition of a point guard.

On the next play, I managed to tip the inbounds pass. Rosa dove to the floor, gathered in the ball and passed it to me. I raced to the basket for a lay up, my first points of the tournament.

"Yes, Brit!" Clarissa shouted. "Up by four!"

We went to a full-court press, but Southern avoided us easily. Cruz caught a pass and put up a three-point shot. Swish!

I heard the game announcer on my way up the court. "What a big shot from Cruz! Southern Maryland is back in the game!"

Up by one, with just a minute left. I bounced the ball to Clarissa. Heather Jackson was in her face immediately, swinging her arms for a steal. There was a flurry of hands, and then the whistle sounded. Clarissa screamed, holding her hand over her right eye.

In one of the worst calls I'd ever seen, the referee whistled for a jump ball. Clarissa had been jabbed in the eye and he was calling a jump ball?! I kept my mouth shut. Ming came onto the floor to replace Clarissa. I tried to put the bad call behind me.

To our dismay, the possession arrow was theirs. Southern brought the ball up and we stiffened our backs. We were anxious to protect our one-point lead. They moved the ball around the perimeter for a while. Finally, with forty seconds left in the game, Sue Whitt flipped the ball to Cruz. She put it up right away. Another three-pointer. Swish!

And just like that, we were down by two. I wasn't going to give up though. I dribbled up-court through heavy pressure from their guards. The announcer's voice was in my ear again, "Little Brittany Bristol," (this had become my nickname), "the sophomore walk-on, is hounded near half-court. She weaves through the defense pretty easily. She's done an excellent job since replacing Kirsten McCann." *Thanks,* I thought.

When I crossed the half-court line, his voice faded. I threw a sharp pass over to Rosa, who quickly threw it in to Ming. She was fouled immediately and went to the line. Ming swished both shots and pulled us back into a tie at 61 all.

"Watch Cruz!" I yelled, as Ming ran by me.

I dogged Whitt, hoping to get my hand on the ball. Somehow, she was able to toss one over to Cruz. Even with a hand in her face, Cruz lit it up with yet another three-pointer. I couldn't believe she hit that one. She was on fire!

We brought the ball back up and Southern fouled Rosa. Even though she made both shots, we were still down one. There were twelve seconds left when Whitt brought the ball up-court. I got position just outside the half-court line. I was forcing Whitt to go around me while Rosa stuck to Cruz like glue. From nowhere, Ming joined me on the double team and slapped the ball away from Whitt. Everyone dove to the floor to retrieve the ball. Somehow, I grabbed it and started dribbling toward their basket. There was nobody between me and an easy lay up. But I'd been so focused on getting that loose ball that I forgot about the clock.

The buzzer sounded before I reached half-court. Southern Maryland advanced and we went home. What followed was a long, hot summer.

CHAPTER TEN

INCH BY INCH

The wind began to blow in from the bay as Brian struggled to weave through the traffic. I had nervously began to flick off my red nail polish with the silver stars.

Brian looked over at me. "Come on," he laughed, "try to think about something else. The streets will be less crowded once we get away from the financial district."

I tried to take my mind off the flashing digital clock on the dashboard. "So," I said, making a conscious effort not to look at the stupid thing, "how long will you be in Bremerton?"

"Until Uncle Sam decides he wants me to go somewhere else," Brian shrugged. "When will you know about the trials?"

"You mean if I even make it to trials?"

"You'll make it. If I have to grab an F-16 and fly you there myself, I will, OK?"

I had to smile. "I should know by the end of the week." I swallowed the remainder of this reply. The reply I'd been telling everyone else in my life. This response usually began with me talking about how nice it was to even be asked to try out. I would then say how I couldn't possibly hope for anything more than the experience of competing. In actuality, this wasn't the truth. "I'd give anything to make the Olympic team," I confided, surprising even myself. I continued, "I mean, representing America would be the chance of a lifetime. Plus, if I make it, a WNBA team is sure to sign me up. Playing basketball as my job," I smiled. "Now that would be something."

"Do you know anybody else going to the WNBA?" Brian asked.

"Yeah, my best friend Clarissa." I paused, "And Sherry Sterling, of course." I groaned.

"Sherry? I don't think so, Brit. Last I heard, she was going to be a teacher."

I felt my face turning bright red. Although I wanted to keep my mouth shut I just couldn't. If Brian wasn't dating her, how on earth did he know so much about her? I had to ask, "So how do you know so much about Sterling?" I was sure our fairy tale day was about to come to an end. Brian was still dating Sherry, or still liked her, anyway. She'd been to visit him at the Naval Academy. They went to prom together. And he knew more about her than I knew about me!

Brian got quiet. "This is a hard thing to talk about."

"I can handle it if you're still dating her. Though, I wish you would have told me earlier."

He cut me off, "I'm not dating her, Brit. I've never dated her." He paused. "I don't know if you know everything about Sherry. Did you know that her mom passed away during her junior year of high school?" Brian's face grew pale.

"No," I answered.

"Well, I got to know Sherry because my mom and her mom were best friends. That's why she and I went to prom together. I knew what a tough time she was having and wanted to help her." His tone lightened, "It all worked out because that's when we met Josh, my roommate at the Academy. After prom, we went to a comedy club and he was there. We hit it off and Josh and I decided to put in a request to be roommates. Josh and Sherry really hit it off. They've been dating ever since. That's why she came up to visit. She was seeing him."

I felt so stupid that I didn't know what to say. "I'm sorry, Brian."

"It's okay. It's just when I said she was misunderstood—" Brian paused. "You know she's got nine younger brothers and sisters to look after? Not *an easy job. That's why there is no WNBA in her future. She can't leave her family. This Olympic team is going to be the end of her basketball career."*

Everything I was learning about Sherry came rushing toward me in a tidal wave. I felt bad about the way I'd treated her. We'd both been chasing the same dream. She'd done nothing wrong, but her dream would soon end. I could talk to my mother whenever I felt like it, but Sherry couldn't. Life seemed pretty unfair, and tears welled up in my eyes. I had misunderstood Sherry. She wasn't mean— she was sad. And she wasn't a dirty player either. She just had more at stake. "Everything makes sense to me now. I owe Sherry an apology."

"Maybe you guys can become friends now and we can double-date." Brian said.

"So, you want to date me now?" I smiled sarcastically.

"Yeah," he said, leaning in to kiss me again.

In my junior season, Coach Hollins appointed me as the starting point guard. I was excited about my new role on the team. I would be sharing the backcourt with Rosa and passing inside to Clarissa. It sounded like a lot of fun.

Our biggest rivals were Virginia Central and my old pal, Sherry Sterling. We faced each other twice, each team winning once at home. We won our conference with Virginia Central right behind us at number two. Not surprisingly, the conference tournament finals found us matched up again. And it was a close game.

With just under six minutes remaining, we were knotted at 55. I brought the ball up and tossed it to Clarissa, who nailed a three-pointer. The UNV students erupted in cheers. That's another good thing about winning——your classmates rally around you.

Up by three with five minutes left, I became too concerned with Starling driving past me. I backpedaled to defend her. The moment the ball touched her hands, she fired a three. I jumped, but wasn't close. Swish! Tie game.

I rushed the ball back up the floor, slinging it over to Jen, who tossed it to Leesha. She put it up from the paint and it bounced off the rim, but Clarissa tapped in the rebound. Back up by two. On the ensuing play, Starling put another shot up the moment she touched the ball. This time, I managed to nip it with my middle finger and knock it off-target. Clarissa leaped into the air and came down with the rebound.

We raced back toward our own goal. Seeing a lane, Clarissa drove hard to the basket. But just as she stepped into the paint, a body flew in from nowhere. Clarissa tripped and fell to the floor hard. We surrounded her instantly. She hugged her knees to her chest, holding her right ankle. The look on her face told me that this was a pretty serious injury. Our trainer came out and helped her up. Then a couple of us assisted her off the court. Since Clarissa couldn't take her foul shots, Coach told me to. I popped them both in. But I was so upset about Clarissa's leg that I could barely see the basket.

Central inbounded the ball with one minute left, down by four. We covered their two guard very closely. She barely got the ball across the half-court line before being called for a ten-second violation. I grabbed for the ball, but she managed to flip it off to Starling. Swish! She never seemed to miss. We led by only two points now.

With fifty seconds left I passed the ball over to Ming. The pass was a little low and Ming never really got control of it. She was easily stripped and we gave chase down the court. I was in Starling's back pocket. When she reached the three-point line, I jumped in front of her. She quickly passed the ball off to a teammate. I watched Karen Lutz chuck a long three-pointer at the hoop. Somehow, it bounced off the backboard and in. No way she meant to do that!

That quickly, we found ourselves down by two with just thirty seconds remaining. I brought the ball up, dribbling patiently as the clock ticked down. I wanted to wait for one final shot to send the game into overtime. Rosa and I exchanged the ball a couple of times. We were trying to get someone open. Finally I set a pick for her and she drove to the lane. She was stopped by three defenders. "Clock!" I shouted as Rosa dribbled near the foul line. There were nine seconds remaining. Immediately, she panicked and fired off a shot from the post. The ball rattled around the rim but didn't fall. Ming was right there to grab the board.

"Three seconds left!" Clarissa screamed from the bench. Quickly, Ming slung the ball out to me at the top of the key. I had no choice but to fire up a long three-pointer. That was not the shot we'd planned for. All eyes were on the ball. It looked to be on line but I couldn't be sure. The buzzer sounded as the ball made a rainbow toward the basket.

A moment later I pumped my fist as the orange leather swished through the net. My first game-winning shot in college! Starling gave me a terrible look as she exited the court, but I just smiled at her. I couldn't have been more excited.

But our celebration was dampened when we learned that Clarissa had gone to the hospital. The next day, our fears were realized. Clarissa had torn her Achilles, ending her season. Hobbling on crutches, she came along with us to the NCAA tournament. We had high hopes that we could survive without our star player. Sadly, we were blown out by Tennessee College in the first round.

Fortunately, Clarissa's Achilles tendon had completely healed by our senior year. We had a great feeling about the year ahead. Our Sunday afternoon get-togethers began the first week of school. We didn't want to waste a second in getting everyone to think as a team.

I had always dreamed of winning a National Championship, but I was realistic about it. After all, UNV had never made it past the second round. But this year felt different somehow. We were a team in every sense of the word and it showed on the court.

Personally, I had a great season. I averaged over fourteen points a game and nearly ten assists. As a team, we lost only four games, winning twenty-one. We entered the conference tournament as the favorite, and we showed everyone why. We blew through everyone, including Sherry Sterling and Virginia Central. It was our second conference championship in a row!

A few weeks later, the NCAA tournament began. Things couldn't have gone better early on. We'd gotten the invite for a third straight year, setting another school record. And somehow, we cruised to victory in both of our first two games. We'd made it to the sweet sixteen for the first time in school history! The sweet sixteen was a really big deal. This was the round in the tournament where only sixteen teams remained from the original sixty-four. Getting there put us two wins away from the Final Four.

When we got on a flight to New Orleans for our game, I was excited. Our game wasn't until the following night. Most of us spent the first day just taking in our surroundings. The spring breeze was warm and gentle as we walked toward the French Quarter. Andrea and Jen tried on one Mardi Gras mask after another. We all lined up to take a streetcar ride.

Meanwhile, I spent a long time outside of an art gallery. I was looking at a painting of a tiny blue dog lost among a crowd of big brown dogs. I know it sounds crazy, but the blue dog reminded me of myself. I was always the blue dog on the basketball court.

When Saturday evening came, I couldn't think about dogs or paintings. All that mattered was the game. Once again, we were happy to be here. After all, we were the lowest-ranked team in the field of sixteen. Still, it was like a dream come true. I couldn't believe how far I'd come since that first time back at Jefferson when I didn't even make the JV team.

Unfortunately, we drew Northern California State, the number one team in the nation. We managed to stay with them early and actually led by one point at halftime. But by the end of the third, we trailed by eight. It was fun while it lasted, and then things got a little ugly. By midway through the fourth quarter, they started wearing us down. Before we knew it, they'd stretched their lead to twenty.

I'd love to tell you that we came back and triumphed, but that isn't what happened. Although we made a decent run in the second half, we came up short and lost. For Clarissa though, the game was a coming-out party. She made some serious noise on one of the last plays of the game. I collected a loose ball and threw a pass to her at the other end of the court. All eyes were on her as she caught the ball and leaped toward the rim. Surprising everyone in the arena, she slammed home a dunk!

The game was on national television, in front of thousands of viewers. The entire place went crazy and it was all anyone could talk about after the game. I think her dunk made more headlines than any other game in the tournament. Needless to say, it was great exposure for her. Everyone in America knew who Clarissa was after that play.

Sure, there were some tears in the locker room after the game. Today was the last game for Clarissa, Ming, Andrea, and I. We'd grown very close in the years we'd played at UNV and now we'd have to move on. It was a bittersweet time in our lives. So we cried for all the good times and the great friends we'd made. Overall, I think we were satisfied. We'd accomplished more than I ever could have dreamed. Two conference titles and a senior season that would go down as the greatest in UNV history! We'd put Northern Virginia on the basketball map. Now everyone had heard of our little school. So when we flew back home the next day, our heads were held high.

CHAPTER ELEVEN

A LONG STRANGE DAY

Brian heaved a deep sigh of frustration. "I should have taken you back to the airport. I was just having so much fun and I wanted you to love San Francisco. I should have——"

I cut him off. "I'm a big girl. I did what I wanted." I was angry with myself. I shouldn't have let this happen. I could see my Olympic dream slipping away. The clock read 5:03. I had twenty-seven minutes before the plane started boarding.

"Nobody could have anticipated an earthquake, right? I'm sure the coach will understand." Brian was trying to convince me that everything would work out.

"She wouldn't understand if the ground opened up and swallowed me whole," I muttered

grimly.

The traffic began to move. "At least then you wouldn't have to worry about being late." He smiled and looked out into the distance. "So tell me, did anybody steal your heart at UNV when I wasn't looking?"

"Some have tried," I said slyly, "but none have succeeded." I didn't tell him that I compared every guy I met to him. I never fell in love with anyone because I was still in love with Brian. I flipped on the radio and we listened to music while holding hands. I thought about how nice it was just to be with him. I almost forgot about the time. Almost.

It was now 5:10. The numbers on the dashboard seemed to get bigger and bigger. "We're not going to make it, are we?" I asked. Reality was starting to set in.

"You bet we are," he responded. And suddenly he swerved the car out of traffic and into a gas station.

"Don't tell me we're out of gas, too." I moaned, the bad luck really getting to me now. Brian didn't answer. He jumped out of the car and raced over to the station attendant. The two of them spoke in the garage for a few seconds. Impatient, I hopped out of the car to see what had gone wrong this time. Brian shook the man's greasy hand and flipped him the keys to the car. I walked a few steps closer to them.

"Helmets?" I heard Brian ask.

"What?" I began.

The man handed us two helmets. I put mine on, completely confused. Then the guy handed us a set of keys. Brian took me by the hand and led me over to a bright blue motorcycle. "Hop on, Brit," he grinned.

Now normally I wouldn't just hop on a motorcycle and start riding into the sunset. This was different, though. I had to get to the airport. As I hopped onto the motorcycle I caught a glance at the words written on the side. Call it coincidence, call it fate, but the motorcycle was called Blue Dog. Right as I read those words I started laughing. Maybe everything would work out.

I hugged Brian tight as he started the engine. He waved to the attendant and yelled over the noisy bike. "I should be back in about an hour. Thank you."

"Thank you," I waved goodbye and held on tight for my first motorcycle ride. Brian drove the big machine along the edge of the roadway and we began to pick up speed. "I think we've got a clear shot to the airport, now," Brian shouted over his shoulder. I tightened my arms around him. We roared away alongside the piled-up cars. My heart was racing almost as fast as the motorcycle. We zipped in between and around the miles of traffic backed up as far as the eye could see. The wind and fog poured in from the ocean and I hugged Brian tighter. In only a

short while, we were on the freeway.

"Not long now," Brian called over his shoulder. The traffic was still heavy but it was moving fairly well.

As we eased off onto the airport exit, I stole a look at my watch, 5:44. The plane was probably getting ready to takeoff. Brian pulled the motorcycle up to the curb and jumped off. "Let's go!" He grabbed my hand and we raced to the ticket counter. I could feel the tears pooling in the corners of my eyes. The terminal clock read 5:49.

"Your ticket, Brit, give him your ticket!" Brian commanded.

I managed to fish the ticket out of my purse, my quick hands suddenly all thumbs. "OK," Brian gushed, pumping the man's hand as he handed me back a stamped ticket. An instant later Brian was pulling me toward the security check. "You got everything?"

I looked at him dumbly. Everything was happening too fast. Finally, I spoke, "My gym bag."

He stopped short. "Where is it?"

"The lockers," I answered.

He looked around quickly and spun me toward the lockers. "Key!" he shouted and I handed it to him. He shoved the key in, but it wouldn't work.

"Try again," I yelled.

He did, but it wouldn't open. "Give me a quarter," he shouted.

"What?" I asked.

"A quarter. If I put another quarter in, it'll open." I searched my pockets and couldn't find one. The clock now read 5:54. Finally, I knew what I had to do. I pulled off my sneaker and grabbed my lucky Washington state quarter. I handed it to Brian. He looked at it for a second before sliding it into the slot. "You're still lucky, Brit, don't worry."

And to be honest, I wasn't. Giving up the quarter that had brought me good luck wasn't a big deal to me. After hearing the story about Sherry Sterling I realized that luck wasn't controlled by quarters. Life wasn't quite that simple. All the lucky quarters in the world wouldn't have cured Mrs. Sterling's cancer.

In an instant, the quarter was a distant memory. Brian jerked out my bag and shoved it into my hands. We raced down the corridor together.

"Last gate," he panted, "wouldn't you know it?"

I grinned, finally realizing I was going to make it to Los Angeles after all.

We reached the end of the tunnel. "Quickly!" the attendant shouted.

Brian pulled me aside before I boarded the plane and kissed me. It was the greatest kiss of my life. It far surpassed the kiss on the observation deck.

"I've missed you, Brian." I whispered against his hair.

Brian smiled. He kissed my hand and let it go.

I raced toward the plane. Just before I disappeared, I heard him shout. "I'll call you every day!"

"Seat 11-A," the young man at the aircraft door said. I hurried in, tossing my gym bag overhead. I collapsed into the seat to fasten my belt as the plane began to pull away from the gate. When I melted into the comfort of that cushion my head was absolutely spinning. My entire life had just been turned upside down. Did I have a boyfriend? Was it Brian? I took a deep breath, forgetting everything. I turned my head to my right and glanced at the passenger in the seat next to me.

In a final twist of fate, I found myself staring into the pretty eyes of Sherry Sterling. As we flew over the tall California mountains, we chatted like old friends. Our rivalry was forgotten as we journeyed together to the next stage. I apologized for the way I acted over the years and she did the same. I told her about Brian. She mentioned that she and Josh had just gotten engaged. Then we both got giddy talking about what it would be like to compete in the Olympics.

I stepped off the plane in Los Angeles and everything had changed. I had Brian. Sherry Sterling and I were friends. I had spent a wonderful day in San Francisco. My life had a clear focus. I was a little blue dog with a great big heart. Was I going to make the Olympic team? Maybe, maybe not. As usual, I was a long shot.

TEST YOURSELF... ARE YOU A PROFESSIONAL READER?

<u>Chapter 1: The List</u>

Name a few reasons why Brittany enjoyed playing point guard.

Explain the differences between Brittany and Clarissa on the basketball court.

How did Brittany stumble upon her love of photography?

<u>ESSAY</u>

In this chapter Brittany tells us that she enjoys the opportunity to be the point guard, the leader on the basketball court. Detail a time in your life when you stepped forward to be a leader. How did that make you feel? Did you learn anything about yourself from this experience?

<u>Chapter 2: A Natural</u>

Who is Susan Ambler? Why doesn't Brittany like her?

How was Brittany's concentration broken during tryouts?

Why did the strongest aspect of Brittany's basketball game abandon her during tryouts? Name that aspect.

ESSAY

In Chapter 2, Brittany is stunned when she fails to make the girls junior varsity basketball team. Detail a disappointment in your life. How did you get over that disappointment? What positives did you take from this experience?

Chapter 3: Layover

What had Brittany done to prepare herself for her second year of junior varsity basketball tryouts?

Why did Brittany pay close attention to the games when she was on the bench?

What did Brian give Brittany before the final cuts for the junior varsity team? Why?

ESSAY

Brittany's actions in this chapter define the word "perseverance." Detail a time in your life when you persevered and overcame odds on your way to success.

Chapter 4: Losing It

What conclusions did Brittany come to after watching her "team" from the bench during the first half of her sophomore year?

Why did Brittany get the opportunity to start the game against Shenendoah?

What thought cheered Brittany up after the game against Shenendoah in which she received a technical foul?

ESSAY

In this chapter, Brittany loses her temper and Coach Holt benches her as a result. Due to her tirade, Brittany doesn't see much more playing time during that season. She eventually realizes that losing her temper didn't help the situation. Detail a time in your life when you lost your temper. Why did you regret the outburst? What did you learn from this incident that helped you in the future?

Chapter 5: Coach Jensen

When Brian and Brittany discuss their high school years, what realization do they make about why they never dated?

What reasoning did Coach Jensen offer to Brittany as to why she would be better suited for another year of junior varsity?

What routine does Brittany's father follow when he is faced with a difficult decision?

ESSAY

In Chapter 5, Brittany dedicates herself and her time to becoming a better basketball player. She reads about the game and practices whenever she can. Detail how reading, knowledge, and hard work will help you as you chase your dream.

Chapter 6: Things Get Ugly

What changes did Brittany help induce in the overall play of Sandi Powers?

Why did Brittany have to wear a "visual appliance" after the game versus Madison?

Why did Brittany receive such anger from her teammates before the big game?

ESSAY

In this chapter, we are given proof that cruel words do hurt. Brittany suffers greatly because of the criticism of her teammates. Describe how Brittany is affected by her teammates' negative comments. What did these words do to her self-confidence?

Chapter 7: Sherry Sterling

Who is Marc Iaccone?

According to Brittany, what aspects of her game set her apart from other talented players across the country?

Despite the reality that no colleges were making a fuss over Brittany Bristol, what recognition off the court marked Brittany as a success?

ESSAY

Throughout this book we learn that Brittany is not a quitter, that she has a strong work ethic and a heart for the game. As you chase your dream, what are some qualities that you have that will enable you to accomplish great things in life?

Chapter 8: Northern Virginia

Why did the "chemistry" in Northern Virginia's locker room begin to further deteriorate when Clarissa Jackson arrived?

What did Clarissa do to try and bridge the gap between her and the rest of the Northern Virginia team?

Why were Brittany and the rest of the freshman class very much looking forward to their sophomore season?

ESSAY

In this chapter, we read about how many of the upperclassmen went out of their way to make newcomer, Clarissa Jackson, feel uncomfortable. They acted this way without even taking the time to get to know her. Name a time in your life when you were guilty of judging someone before you actually took the time to know them.

What did this teach you?

Chapter 9: Sophomore Year

Why did Brittany enjoy her job working as a counselor at a basketball camp during the summer before her sophomore year?

Despite not being in the starting lineup, why did Brittany consider her sophomore season a success?

Why did UNV's excitement wane when they walked onto the floor for their game against Southern Maryland?

ESSAY

Something as simple as Sunday evening cookie parties obviously helps UNV's team chemistry and camaraderie. The girls grow to become friends outside of the basketball court. Why would this friendship and closeness help a team play better basketball? Detail some differences between the UNV team during Brittany's freshman and sophomore seasons.

Chapter 10: Inch by Inch

How had Brittany misunderstood Sherry Sterling? What didn't Brittany know about Sherry's personal life?

What situation put a damper on UNV's victory over Virginia Central?

How did UNV fare in the NCAA tournament during Brittany's junior season?

ESSAY

In this chapter we are aware of the bittersweet time in Brittany's life, and in all the lives of her senior teammates as they prepare to leave college. Brittany and her teammates are torn between moving on with their lives and remembering all the great times they had in college. Detail a time in your life when "moving on" was bittersweet. How did this experience make you feel?

Chapter 11: A Long, Strange Day

Why did Brittany laugh when she hopped onto the motorcycle with the words "'Blue Dog'" written on the side?

Why did Brittany have to give up her lucky quarter?

What in Brittany's life had changed when she stepped off the plane in Los Angeles?

ESSAY

Congratulations! You have completed another Scobre book. What did you learn from Brittany's life and the way in which she chased her dreams? How do you plan on making your dreams come true?